PRIME TIME LOVE

THE 1ST ABIGAIL LOVE BOOK AND THE VERY BEST IN FUNNY BRITISH LAUGH OUT LOUD ROMANTIC COMEDY CHIC LIT ROM COM STORY TYPE THINGS

David Blake

www.david-blake.com

Edited and proofread by Lorraine Swoboda

Published in Great Britain, 2017

Disclaimer:
These are works of fiction. Names, characters, businesses, places, events and incidents are either the products of the author's imagination or used in a fictitious manner. Any resemblance to actual persons, living or dead, or actual events is purely coincidental.

ISBN: 9781520431918

DEDICATION

For Akiko, Akira and Kai.

BOOKS BY DAVID BLAKE

THE ABIGAIL LOVE SERIES

1. Prime Time Love
2. Headline Love

THE INSPECTOR CAPSTAN SERIES:

1. The Slaughtered Virgin of Zenopolis
2. The Curious Case of Cut-Throat Cate
3. The Thrills & Spills of Genocide Jill
4. The Herbaceous Affair of Cocaine Claire

CONTENTS

DAVID BLAKE

ACKNOWLEDGMENTS

I'd like to thank my family for putting up with me and my rather odd sense of humour.

I'd also like to thank my Editor and Proofreader, Lorraine Swoboda, for making sure that what I write makes sense, sort of, and that all the words are in the right order.

I also need to say huge thank you to The Book Club (TBC) on Facebook, for their dedication, hard work and support towards helping author members succeed.

CHAPTER ONE
I've ALWAYS BEEN FASCINATED BY THE NEWS

'SO, RICHARD…Wankett, is it?' asked a well-groomed middle-aged man sitting behind a large opaque glass desk, with a creased tanned face, a pressed white shirt and a stripy blue tie.

'Er, yes. But I prefer to use my middle name,' answered a much younger, good-looking sort of a chap sitting opposite, wearing a similar white shirt but sporting a mustard yellow tie.

'I see. And your middle name is Will?' asked the man behind the desk again, as he considered the CV in front of him.

'Short for William,' answered the younger one.

'So, your full name, as it's written here, is therefore, er, Richard Will Wankett?' and the man stared up at the chap opposite with a bemused look of pity.

'That's right,' answered Will, who was beginning to feel increasingly uncomfortable.

'But - wouldn't you prefer to be called by your first name?'

'Well, yes. And I did try that when I started going to school, but the moment everyone found out what my surname was, they just shortened it to Dick.'

'Which would make it Dick Will Wankett,' summarised the man who was supposed to be conducting a job interview, but seemed unable to move beyond the subject of the candidate's name.

'Yes, that probably *is* worse,' he added, as he began to wonder if he could really employ someone whose name sounded like a 19th Century steam-powered wanking machine, one that may have been invented by a chap called Richard, and specifically for members of the male population who'd possibly had the misfortune to lose their right hand due to a work-related accident. 'Have you never considered using the name William, instead of Will?' he asked.

'I have, of course,' answered Will, unsure why he was being forced to have such a personal conversation with someone he'd only met about thirty seconds earlier, especially when the only other people he'd discussed the problem with in such depths before were his mum and his NHS child psychologist, both when going through puberty. 'But the same thing happens,' he continued. 'And at the end of the day, I'd rather be known as a Will than a Dick.'

'Fair enough,' said the interviewer, and was about to suggest that he tried the name Bill instead of Will when he realised just how red the young man's face had become, and forced himself to apologise and move on.

'Sorry about all that. It's just that it certainly is, well, it could be considered by some to be a remarkably unusual name.'

Will just shrugged. He'd had it all his life, as had everyone in his family, so for him it seemed quite normal.

'Anyway, my name's Eliot Bespoke,' announced the man behind the desk, and to help lighten the mood a little added, 'which I suppose is quite uncommon in itself!'

The young man opposite still looked hopelessly embarrassed, so Eliot decided to completely change the subject.

'Let me tell you a little about Hampshire Today. As I'm sure you're aware, we're a relatively new local YouTube news channel that I started about four months ago. So, as you can imagine, we're still finding our feet. And despite having had a recent exclusive scoop with the Portsmouth Prison story, I consider us to be very much a start-up company, albeit a successful one.'

Eliot Bespoke was now staring directly at Will Wankett, as if expecting some sort of verbal response. But the only thing Will could think to say was, 'Well done!' which somehow didn't seem appropriate.

'It's for that reason,' continued Eliot, 'that I remain very much a hands-on member of the team and, for now at least, serve as the Director of News, Media & Current Affairs. So, were you to join us, you'd be effectively working under me, although not directly.'

Once more Eliot stared over at Will, who again felt obliged to say something in response, so he said, 'That sounds great!' even though it didn't.

Deciding to re-examine the young man's CV, Eliot said, 'Maybe we can kick things off by asking why it is that you'd like to work for us?'

Will had been expecting that question, and came straight out with his pre-prepared answer.

'Because I think it sounds like a very exciting opportunity.'

'For you or for me?' mused Eliot, with a wry smile.

He'd always had rather a dry sense of humour, which few people seemed to understand, let alone appreciate.

'Er…for me,' answered Will, but then realised that may have sounded a little selfish, so he added, 'Although I'm sure it's a great opportunity for you as well, Mr Eliot, sir.'

'And why's that, do you think?'

'Um, because, er…you get to run your own news channel?'

'No, sorry, I meant why do you think it would be a good opportunity for *you*?'

'Oh, well, er…because I'd get to work for Hampshire Today, which I've no doubt would be very exciting.' Relieved to have been able to come up with some sort of an answer, he gave his potential new boss a victorious sort of a grin.

Eliot picked up Will's CV from his desk and leant back in his black executive's chair, glancing down the single page document. He turned it over to see if there was anything written on the back, but there wasn't.

'It's a little on the short side for a CV, wouldn't you say?' he asked, more as a point of observation than anything else.

'Is it?' responded Will. He knew it was, but he'd never been much of one for writing, which was odd, given his chosen profession of journalism.

'You'd better tell me a little more about yourself, then.'

Will didn't like talking much either, especially about himself, and certainly not during a job interview. He considered himself to be more of a thinking man's man, which basically meant that he was what society labelled an introvert, but for him it felt more like having some sort of a personality disorder. What it did mean was that when forced to talk in front of people, especially those he hardly knew, he had a tendency to start babbling.

'I was born on 10th May, 1989,' he began, 'which makes me twenty seven. I grew up in Gosport, just down the road from here. My father was a vicar, but passed away a few years back. My mother's a teacher, or at least she was. She's retired now, and spends most of her time either knitting, reading psychological thrillers, or listening to Radio 4. I have a brother and a sister, both older. One of them lives in Surrey, and the other in Gloucester. My brother's an occupational therapist and my sister's a graphic designer. They're both married with children of their own. My first school was Whitworth, Church of England. I was there until I was about eight, I think, which was when I moved up into…'

'Sorry,' interrupted Elliot, 'but I was really hoping that you could tell me a little more about the history of your employment?'

'Oh, right! Well I suppose my first job,' began Will again, 'was washing my Dad's car. He used to pay me one pound every time I did it, so I used to do it quite a lot. I also got a pound whenever I cut the grass, but that was before I got a paper-round, which I got £5 for and took half the time, and allowed me to save up for a…'

'I meant,' interrupted Eliot again, 'about your *recent* work experience, since you graduated?'

'I thought that was on my CV?' asked Will, feeling

as if the man was deliberately trying to make him look like he was a biscuit short of a tin.

Eliot glanced back down at the document. The job that Will had been doing since graduating was, of course, written down there. But Eliot had been hoping to find out a little more about what that job entailed.

'It says that you're currently working as a journalist for the Portsmouth Post.'

'That's correct,' answered Will, 'although that CV's a little out of date now.'

'Oh really? How come?'

'I was made redundant on Friday.'

'I see,' said Eliot. 'For any particular reason?'

'General staff cutbacks,' he answered. 'Since becoming a free paper a few years back, they've been struggling.'

That didn't surprise Eliot, and the general decline of the local newspaper industry was one of the reasons why he'd started up a YouTube news channel instead. News was all about visual entertainment now, and much less about the written word. But despite that, he still felt that the job applicant sitting in front of him should have made an effort to write a few more.

'So,' continued Eliot, 'you have a degree in Media Studies, and have five years' experience of working as a journalist for the Portsmouth Post. But we're a television news channel, which is a completely different kettle of fish.'

Will had no idea what a kettle filled up with fish had to do with anything, but could already sense that the interview wasn't going well. However, being in debt by over £5,000, with his credit card maxed out and his rent overdue, he was desperate, and felt that if he didn't get this job, then he'd be forced to move back in with his mum, something he'd do almost anything to avoid.

'Yes, but I've always been fascinated by the news,' he said, in his own defence, 'and I watch it nearly every day!'

But Eliot had become distracted by a young lady who'd just breezed past the window he used mainly to keep an eye on his minions in the smaller than average open-plan office beyond.

'Hold on a sec, will you?' he said to Will, as he stood up from behind his desk to walk over to his office door. Pulling it open he called out, 'Abigail! Abigail! Can you come in here for a minute please?'

Leaving the door open, he returned to his seat. 'Sorry about this,' he said, 'but it won't take a minute.'

CHAPTER TWO
A POOR WARDROBE CHOICE

L OCAL GIRL Abigail Love, another Media Studies graduate who'd spent five years working as an Editorial Research Assistant for BBC South East before taking a gamble with Hampshire Today, wasn't in a good mood. Yes, she'd been fortunate enough to land the story the week before of the Portsmouth Prison riots that saw twenty nine prison guards being hurled over the walls to their certain deaths, and yes, she'd picked up some half-decent commission when Eliot had managed to sell her exclusive news footage to both BBC and Sky News for a handsome sum. But then she'd been forced to make camp outside the prison for four days, along with what felt like the entire nation's press, in what Eliot called their Mobile Communications Satellite Earth Station, but which was basically a beaten-up old Volkswagen camper van with a TV satellite dish stuck on its roof.

And up to a point, that was all fine, as it was an expected part of the job. However, she'd had to spend that time effectively shacked up with her cameraman, a retired factory worker called Herman, who'd been forced back into the workplace to help pay for his ongoing drinking problem.

Eliot had employed Herman not only because he was cheap, which he was, obviously, but because his hobby was the making and production of home movies. For those, Herman had gained some local notoriety, winning Portsmouth Post's Amateur Film of the Year Award 2008 for his re-make of the science fiction action-packed blockbuster, *Jumper*. The year after that he'd won it again for coming up with a credible sequel he'd called *Cardigan*, and again the following year for the third instalment, *Pullover*. However, his remake of the 1997 American post-apocalyptic epic that originally starred Kevin Costner, called *The Postman*, didn't fare so well. Local critics said that it bore no resemblance to the original film, probably because it simply featured his own postman, doing his rounds. After his next project, *The Milkman*, fared far worse, he hit the bottle hard, and not one that contained any milk. A few weeks later he was fired for turning up to work every day drunk, and after a number of years of unemployment he'd almost given up hope, when he saw an ad in the local Job Centre for an experienced cameraman.

For Abigail, that simply meant that she'd been stuck with a decrepit old alcoholic who had a permanent aroma of urine and whisky that seemed to become more pronounced every day, Monday to Friday, from ten o'clock onwards. To be enclosed inside a camper van with him for four days in a row was above and beyond the call of duty.

On top of that, her overtly possessive boyfriend had had a fit of jealousy. He'd never met Herman before, but just the idea of her sleeping within such close proximity to another man had sent him over the edge, and, unable to cope, he'd dumped her mid-week, by text.

But the icing on the cake had been when she'd been

dragged, kicking and screaming, out of their news van by several burly men in the middle of the night, all wearing suits that looked like they dated back to the 1970's, and which clearly were far too tight a fit, even by modern day standards. The dodgy-looking men had taken it upon themselves to tie her up next to Herman, along with all the other journalists who'd been camped outside the prison walls, where she'd had no choice but to remain for several hours before being discovered by a stray dog with the name Pencil Case attached to its collar. Fortunately, for all of them, the dog was able to raise the alarm by barking incessantly for about half an hour until an early morning jogger found them and alerted the police.

Hearing her boss, Eliot Bespoke, calling out her name behind her, twice, as she attempted to slink past his office window without being noticed, she already had a pretty good idea what he wanted to moan at her about. The fact that Herman and she had been incapacitated, otherwise known as tied up, meant that she'd missed the second biggest story of the year, for Portsmouth at least. That was what the British media had elected to call *The Battle of the Isle of Wight*, which was when the small island lying just off Hampshire's coast had been taken over by the entire population of Portsmouth Prison later that very same day, and by the very same dangerous criminals who'd lent a malevolent hand in tying her up.

Her only saving grace was that at least nobody else had managed to get the story, but she was still expecting to get a verbal roasting over having missed it.

Stopping dead in her tracks and cursing her morning's wardrobe choice of a bright red tie-collar blouse that she should have known would have been spotted from half a mile away, Abigail took a calming intake of breath, spun around and headed for his door.

'You wanted to see me, Eliot?' she asked from the doorway.

'Yes. Hello, Abigail. I was just wondering if there'd been any news on that missing escaped convict?'

'You mean the head of the Centre for Organised Crime and Kidnapping, Morose?'

'Yes, that one?'

'No, nothing yet.'

'I see. And what about that injured police detective chap?'

'Inspector Capstan? The last I heard he'd slipped into a coma, but I'm waiting for Herman to show up so that we can head down to the hospital to find out the latest.'

'Is Herman *still* not in?' asked Eliot, glancing down at his watch.

'I'm afraid not, but saying that, he really didn't look too good when I saw him last.' In an optimistic tone, she added, 'He's probably dead.'

Eliot, fortunately, shared her desire that Herman may have passed away during the course of the weekend.

Only about a week after employing him he'd known he'd made a mistake. Apart from the fact that he never seemed able to show up for work before ten o'clock, and when he did he smelled of urine or whisky, or both, the film footage he'd taken never seemed to be in focus. It had also been shaky and badly framed, but Eliot didn't mind that so much, as it had helped to add drama to the footage. The continued tardiness, the smell, and the man's inability to use the camera's focus control had left Eliot looking for a good enough reason to fire him; but to do that he'd need to have another cameraman at hand, ready to step into his shoes, so to speak. That would mean employing someone else, and his fixed overheads were already quite high enough without having yet another employee on his books.

He had an idea, and looked at the young man still sitting in front of him, who'd continued to face forwards during the conversation with Abigail.

'I don't suppose you can use a video camera?' he asked, glancing back down at the CV.

'What, you mean like an iPhone?' asked Will.

Eliot fairly obviously hadn't meant that, but it wasn't a bad idea. In the right hands, it would probably still take better footage than what Herman had achieved with their brand new Sony XDCAM PXW-Z100 system. And besides, if Inspector Capstan had woken from his coma, he couldn't risk missing another big story.

'Have you got one?' he asked.

'Yes. It's actually the latest,' Will answered, as he pulled it out from his inside suit jacket pocket.

'Right. I'll make a deal with you,' said Eliot. 'If you can spend the day with Abigail here, and bring back some decent footage on your phone, then I'll give you the job of cameraman. How about it?'

'Er,' said Will, as he turned to glance behind him at

the Abigail being referred to.

The lady looked strangely familiar, but it wasn't from her recent appearances on the local news, as he hardly ever watched it, either on TV or YouTube. He'd definitely seen her before somewhere, but for the life of him couldn't remember where. But despite that, and the fact that she was a visually stunning dark-haired young lady with blue eyes and smooth, silken white skin, he turned back to Eliot and said, 'But I came for a job as a news correspondent!'

'Tell you what, if you do this, we'll think about promoting you. What do you say?' and Eliot stood up from behind his desk, held out his hand and gave Will a beaming great smile in a bid to seal the deal.

By that time Will had been able to put the two main pieces of the offer together in his head, those being that he'd just been invited to spend the day following someone around who just happened to be one of the most attractive girls he'd met, or was about to, in a very long time, and the other being that he was going to get paid to do it.

'I accept!' he said, and rose to shake his new boss by the proffered hand.

'Good man, well done!' said Eliot, and walked around his desk to make the necessary introductions.

'Abigail, meet Will. Will, meet Abigail.'

CHAPTER THREE
Clandestine Reminiscence

WHILE WILL OCCUPIED himself in trying to work out how to take a video with his new iPhone, Abigail sat behind the wheel of Hampshire Today's news van as they headed for Portsmouth Hospital to find out if local police hero Inspector Capstan had yet emerged from his coma.

Abigail had elected not to keep an eye on the story over the weekend, as she felt she was due a couple of days off, but after her meeting with Eliot she'd phoned the hospital to hear that the police hero was still unconscious, and so, as was often the case when living in Portsmouth, she hadn't missed much. But now that she was back on the story, and knowing that the man could wake up at any moment and start blabbing to the very first journalist he happened to lay eyes on, she was keen to get down there as soon as possible.

Apart from Will pondering his iPhone's video functionality settings, and Abigail wondering if news vans fell under the same category as taxis when it came to using a bus lane, and if not, who'd get the fixed penalty charge, herself or Eliot, there was something else playing on both their minds. It was a question that neither seemed prepared to bring up; that they both had a strong sense of already knowing each other. However, neither could be certain, and if they could, had no idea from where.

Being journalists by trade, even if one of them was

more of a thinking man's one, they were each trying to come up with a question that would firstly help to break the ice, as they'd yet to exchange more than two words since meeting, and secondly, to find out where it might be that they knew each other from.

First to have a go was Abigail.

'Are you from around here?'

'Oh, um…I was born…' began Will, but with determined mental effort forced himself not to launch into yet another rendition of his life story, as fascinating as he thought it was. Instead he simply continued by saying, 'not far from here,' and after a momentary pause, had the good sense to knock the question straight back to her. 'And you?'

'Portsmouth,' she answered. 'Well, Gosport to be precise, but it's close enough.'

That innocent piece of information was enough for Will to remember exactly who Abigail was, and where they had met. Her full name was Abigail May Love, and they'd been in the same class together at Whitworth School, right up until taking their GCSEs. And although for most men discovering that the attractive young lady sitting within snogging distance of them was an old childhood girl-chum, so giving them the perfect opportunity to get to know each other all over again, but in a far more grown-up sort of a way that could easily involve a romantic dinner for two, followed by doing it doggy-style in the back of a car, it had quite the opposite effect on Will. This was because throughout most of his time at school, Abigail Love, who he used to refer to as Fanny-Gail the Horrible, was Public Enemy Number One, his nemesis, his most bitter playground rival; a girl who seemed to deliberately want to make his life a living hell on a daily basis, and apparently all because of his surname.

Abigail was still clueless to the fact that the attractive young man blessed with a full head of dark hair, intelligent brown eyes and boyish good looks, who'd just been appointed her new cameraman for the day, hopefully longer, was in fact the very child who she used to tease as often as possible at school. This had begun at the beginning of the very first day of Year 7, when she'd started to call him *Wee Willy Wankett,* which she'd follow up by asking, "Where's your blankett, Wee Willy Wankett?" for no other reason than the word "blankett" rhymed with Wankett, and back then she'd yet to learn the word most adults would associate with such an unusual surname.

However, as is often the case at such a young age, it made more sense for her to torment the boy into a series of child counselling sessions than to admit to him, and therefore everyone else at the school, her true feelings. After all, at the time they were both adolescents of the opposite sex, attempting to come to terms with their increasing needs for carnal stimulation, but without the necessary social tools to reach a point beyond being sexually frustrated on a seemingly unending basis. And as at the time she had bad skin, yellow teeth and NHS glasses, she used the public ridicule of any boy she happened to fancy as a justifiable self-defence mechanism, to protect her from the rejection she thought would be sure to follow were that person to discover how she really felt.

It wasn't until she went to sixth form college that she transformed into the radiant beauty she was today, something she'd managed to achieve by maintaining a more healthy diet, having her teeth whitened, joining a gym, the liberal use of makeup, buying some curling tongs, swapping glasses for contact lenses, the purchase of a number of push-up bras and tight-fitting blouses, and starting to amass what had since become an impressive collection of shoes.

'And what did you do, before, er…this?' she asked.

The question snapped Will out of the trance-like state he'd slipped in to as he'd begun to mentally re-visit those torturous days back in the school playground, and he gave her a sideways glance.

Catching his eye she returned a perfect smile that was graced with immaculate teeth and sumptuous red lips.

His body churned with emotions. My God, she was attractive, he admitted; but it was the same girl. There was no doubt about that!

He eventually came out with, 'I worked for the Portsmouth Post, as a reporter.'

'Oh right! I was thinking about applying for a job there myself,' answered Abigail in a relaxed, conversational tone, 'but I got a job offer from the BBC soon after graduating. I only worked there as an Editorial Research Assistant, which was hardly what I wanted to do, which was why I applied for the job at Hampshire Today.'

It was then that Will realised that he seemed to have found himself in an advantageous position, for him at least. He'd recognised her, but as far as he could make out, she was none the wiser as to who he was. That was hardly surprising. It must have been well over ten years since they'd last seen each other, and he knew that his own physical appearance had changed considerably since then. There was just a vague possibility that, were he to somehow prevent her from discovering what his surname was, she might continue to be ignorant of the fact, at least long enough for him to exact some sort of revenge for a childhood of prolonged embarrassment and untold misery.

CHAPTER FOUR
BOB, SHORT FOR ANDREW

THE CONVERSATION pretty much ended there, and after stopping off at a garage, from which Abigail emerged wearing a pair of aviator sunglasses and carrying a bunch of flowers, they continued on to Portsmouth Hospital, found somewhere to park, climbed down from the van and walked over towards the main entrance.

As they approached, she said, 'Actually, it may be a real advantage that you don't have a TV camera. Thinking about it, it probably was always a bit of a giveaway that we were from a television news channel, especially as it has *Hampshire Today* written all over it. You never know, if we play our cards right, we may even be able to sneak into Inspector Capstan's private room and land some sort of exclusive interview.'

'Oh, OK,' answered Will, before realising that there was rather an obvious stumbling block to her plan. 'But I thought he was still in a coma?'

'Who knows?' replied Abigail. 'Maybe he is, and maybe he isn't. He could easily have woken up by now, and as I can't see any other news vans around, it may be our lucky day! The main problem will be to find a way into his private room. The last time I was here, they'd stuck a policeman right outside the door. So, if we're to have any chance of a story, we're going to need a way in.'

'Yes, but what if we manage to get in, and he's still

21

in a coma?' asked Will. 'Wouldn't it make more sense if we found out what his condition was before trying to interview him?'

'That sort of attitude may have worked for a local paper like the Portsmouth Post, but you're in prime time telly-land now, where everything moves along just a little bit faster.'

'But, surely, if he's in a coma, he's in a coma,' said Will, in defence of his own argument. 'And although there's research suggesting that those in such a condition are able to hear some of what's going on around them, I've never heard one to be up for an in-depth television interview before.'

It was an obvious point, but largely irrelevant to an opportunistic journalist like Abigail.

'You're not one of those people who sees the glass as being half empty, I hope?' she asked.

'Not at all! I'm just suggesting that it may be better to wait until he comes out of his coma before trying to land an exclusive interview.'

'Let me ask you this,' she continued, as they approached the entrance. 'Before you set off for work each day, do you wait until all the traffic lights are green?'

At some point Will must have read the same self-help book from which Abigail had extracted that nugget of infinite wisdom, and answered, 'No, but I've got a bicycle, so I don't have to.'

Abigail could feel an altercation brewing that, knowing her, could easily lead to a full-blown argument. But as she'd only met the man half an hour earlier, and as she'd reached the conclusion that he was cute the moment they'd met, and had therefore already imagined spending two years dating the guy, walking down the aisle with him, having three children by him, and moving into an impressive Edwardian detached house in Surrey shortly afterwards, one that was set within a large private estate that boasted a fountain and easy access to Oxford Street, she made a concerted effort to be *nice*. With that in mind, she said, 'At least you have a sense of humour!'

'I wasn't joking,' he answered. 'I have got a bicycle.'

She gave him a quick sideways glance in a bid to try and work out if he was being serious, or was still pushing on with the same joke, being that he had a particularly dry sense of humour like Eliot's. However, from his facial expression, it was impossible to tell.

'Anyway,' she said, 'the problem is that we don't have much of a choice. If he's still in a coma, then he could be for months on end, by which time the story would be dead, even if he wasn't. And as good stories don't grow on trees, not around here at any rate, we have to make the best of what we've got.'

Despite the premise that it was unlikely that an interview with someone in a coma would make for great TV, even by today's standards, she'd made some valid points. So Will decided not to raise any more objections, for now, and to just wait and see how the situation played itself out.

Pushing their way through the glass swing doors, Abigail held the flowers firmly in front of her and, without warning, looped her arm around Will's.

Instinctively he flinched, and tried to pull his own away, leading Abigail to almost say, 'Steady there, boy,' as if he was a horse being introduced to its new owner. But instead she said, 'Just follow my lead, and try to look as if you may be about to lose someone very close to you.'

'Why, where are you going?' he asked, with one of his wry smiles. But he got the idea and relaxed a little, and although unsure if he could pull off the sort of look she was referring to, that of wistful grief, he knew he could at least do perpetual disappointment, as that was his general outlook on life, and it was close enough that he didn't think anyone would notice.

Avoiding the reception desk ahead, Abigail led Will straight over to the elevator doors, which happened to ping open in front of them. After waiting patiently for an elderly couple to shuffle their way out, they stepped inside.

'He's on the 3rd floor,' she said to Will, with a nod down at the buttons that were laid out on his side of the lift.

Pressing the relevant one, it wasn't long before the doors pinged open again and Abigail led Will out, and down a quiet beige-carpeted corridor.

Ahead they could see a policeman in full uniform sitting outside a room, gently sipping at a cup of something hot, with a black clipboard resting on his lap.

'*That's the one,*' she whispered, and tightened her arm around Will's. '*Now, let me do the talking, OK?*'

Will didn't have a problem with that. He'd no idea what to say under such circumstances.

As they approached, Abigail called out, 'Excuse me?'

The policeman looked up and then stood, clipboard in one hand, coffee in the other. 'May I help you?'

'We've come to see Inspector Capstan,' continued Abigail. 'Is this the right room?'

'Yes, but unfortunately we're only allowing family members in,' and he glanced down at the clipboard where she could see was a printed list of names.

'Oh, we are related,' she said. 'I'm his niece and this,' glancing at Will beside her, 'is his nephew.'

'And your names?' asked the policeman, not looking particularly convinced.

'I'm Abigail and this is Will.'

Having glanced down the list he looked up at them again through narrowing eyes, and asked, 'And what's your uncle's name?'

'Sorry,' answered Abigail, feeling Will's arm tense up against hers. 'How d'you mean?'

'Well, you've just asked to see a patient by the name of Inspector Capstan, which, if you'll excuse me for saying so, does seem a little odd, being that you're supposed to be his niece and nephew. I'd have thought that, if you were indeed his niece and nephew, as you say you are, that you would have asked for him by name, and not rank.'

'Yes, of course,' said Abigail, letting slip a nervous laugh. 'That was silly of me,' and in a bid to change the subject, smiled at him and asked, 'And what's *your* name?'

But the policeman wasn't going to be so easily side-tracked.

'Never you mind what my name is, young lady, but I'm certainly curious to see if you know the full name of the patient you'd like to see.'

'Er, well, we just call him Uncle, obviously,' she answered. 'Although we sometimes call him Unc', for short.'

'I see,' said the policemen, and brought his clipboard up to his chest so that they couldn't see what was written on it. 'And just out of interest,' he said, staring at them both with clear suspicion, 'what is your uncle's *first* name?'

'Bob!' answered Abigail, that being the first one that came into her head.

The policeman eased his clipboard away from his chest to check the answer, and then looked back at Abigail.

'It says Andrew here.'

'Yes, that's right. But his family calls him Bob.'

'Right. And why do you call him Bob when his name is actually Andrew?'

'It's a long story,' replied Abigail, and not too keen to start having to make it up, continued, 'but we're both on our lunch break, and so we really don't have very long. Is it all right if we just pop in and see him, please?' and she gave him her most vivacious smile.

'Well, OK, you can go in, but only for a few minutes. Is that understood?'

'Fully, thank you, Constable,' she said. 'That's most kind of you.' Then she gave Will an affectionate nudge in the ribs, and said, 'Come on Will, let's go and see how Uncle Bob's getting along.'

CHAPTER FIVE
IS ANYBODY IN THERE?

CLOSING THE DOOR behind them, they both took a moment to take in their new surroundings. On a single bed, over to the right-hand side of what was a fairly small room, was a distinctly French-looking chap. He was tucked under a pristine white bedsheet, on top of which was spread a smooth, wrinkle-free navy blue blanket. The man's arms lay either side of him, on top of the blanket, and his head was turned up towards the ceiling, his eyes closed.

Against the far wall stood various medical apparatuses, one of which bleeped out his heart beat in a steady enough rhythm. The other was an intravenous drip that had a clear plastic tube leading from a suspended bag of fluids all the way down to the man's left arm, where the end disappeared under a single piece of surgical tape.

But of most interest, to Abigail at least, was a bunch of flowers, tulips to be precise, nestled in a glass vase on the bedside table. They looked long past their sell by date, so she took them out, dumped them into a nearby bin, and replaced them with the ones she'd picked up on the way over there.

Having watched the man in the bed for any signs of conscious life, Will asked, 'So, what do you think?'

'I think they're beautiful, don't you?' she said, as she began to arrange them in the vase.

'Er, no. I meant about that man lying there,' and

27

Will pointed at the inanimate form in an effort to remind Abigail of the primary purpose for their unauthorised clandestine visit. 'Do you think he's just asleep?'

Abigail pulled herself away from the flowers to stare down at the person in question.

'He could be,' she said, 'but either way, we need to find out.'

Setting her handbag down beside the vase, she moved over to the patient. Resting both her hands on his shoulders, she began shaking him with some vigour, shouting, 'MR CAPSTAN? HELLO? CAN YOU HEAR ME?' directly at his face.

What the hell do you think you're doing?' whispered Will, through his teeth, as he glanced around at the door. Not only was he appalled by such a blatant act of disrespect, but she was making a hell of a noise.

'I'm *trying* to wake him up, *obviously*!' she replied, before carrying on.

'INSPECTOR? HELLO? IS ANYBODY IN THERE?'

'For Christ's sake, Abigail, the man's clearly still in a coma, and I'm really not convinced that shaking him until his eyes fall out is going to make any difference!'

'Crap!' she said, reaching the same conclusion. 'Looks like it's Plan B then.'

But Will didn't even know that there'd been a Plan A, unless she was referring to the one where they'd pretended to be a private patient's relatives in order to talk their way past a policeman, and so giving them an exclusive opportunity to change the man's flowers. With that in mind, he asked, 'Sorry, what's Plan B?'

'We'll just have to interview him as he is.'

'I see,' said Will, struggling to understand how she was going to do that.

Abigail seemed to have already thought it through, and removed the aviator sunglasses, the same ones she'd bought with the flowers, from off the top of her head where they'd been perched, and eased them onto the coma victim's face.

When they were positioned as they were supposed to be - propped up on the bridge of his nose with the metal arms tucked behind his ears - she heaved the man's head forward, along with his upper torso, to re-arrange the pillows behind him.

'Get your phone ready. I doubt we'll have time for more than one take.'

She eased the man back down onto the now plumped-up pillows, moved his arms so that they rested naturally in his lap, and stood back to admire her work.

'What d'ya reckon?' she asked.

'Well, yes. He looks like a man sitting up in a hospital bed, wearing a pair of sunglasses which, frankly, looked better on you. But I still remain fascinated to see how you're going to make his mouth move up and down at the same time as words come out of it.'

'Don't worry about that,' she said, as she opened her generously-proportioned handbag to pull out a large microphone. 'Just concentrate on getting your iPhone ready.'

With the mic lodged under her chin, she dived back into her bag to root around for her compact and her lipstick. Finding both, she returned the bag to the bedside table, opened the small round mirror, gave her face a quick once-over, and closed the compact to dump that and the lipstick back into the bag. Swinging around she looked up at Will, and asked, 'How do I look?' while using her free hand to give her hair a last minute prod.

'Well, you look fine, but I'm really not sure...'

'And my hair?' she interrupted.

As far as Will could tell, her hair looked the same as it had done before: long, dark and a bit straggly, so having to assume that was the look she was going for, said, 'It's fine, but I still don't understand what you two are going to talk about, being that one of you seems to be in a perpetual dream-like state - although, to be honest, I'm becoming a bit confused as to which one of you that is.'

'It really isn't that complicated,' she said, in a condescending tone. 'We can simply overlay him talking when we get back to the office.'

'Ah, of course!' said Will, with a thick layer of sarcasm. 'Now why didn't I think of that?'

Ignoring him, Abigail asked, 'Are you ready?

'Well, I suppose so.'

'What about your iPhone?'

He'd forgotten all about that, so he quickly pulled it out from his inside suit jacket pocket, turned it on and held it out so that it was horizontally positioned facing Abigail and the guy propped up in the bed next to her.

'Can you see both of us?' she asked, holding her microphone up to her mouth.

'Well, yes,' he replied. 'You're both in the frame,

but you won't be needing the mic. I've got no way of plugging it into my phone, and besides, the inbuilt one on this will do the job.'

'It's just a prop. They rarely work.' And without further ado, she announced, 'OK, let's go!'

Standing beside the bed, she shook her hair out, licked her immaculate white teeth and stared over at Will's iPhone.

'Is it on?' she asked.

'It's filming, yes,' replied Will.

'Right,' and after a long intake of breath, she began.

'This is Abigail Love reporting from Portsmouth Hospital. With me today is local hero, Inspector Andrew Capstan of the Solent Police, who's agreed to give Hampshire Today an exclusive interview.'

'Mr Inspector Capstan,' she said, as she half-turned towards the man propped-up in the bed with the sunglasses that successfully disguised the fact that his eyes were still firmly closed, 'thank you so much for agreeing to talk to me. Now, I understand you've been through quite a harrowing time. I know it may be difficult for you, but would it be possible to tell us, in your own words, exactly what happened; especially the bit about when you went head to head with the criminal mastermind, Morose?'

She held her microphone over the man's mouth in such a way as to prevent Will's iPhone from recording the fact that no part of it was actually moving in response to her question. And after a few moments of silence, she pulled the mic back, and asked, 'And what happened then?'

She repeated the process before saying, 'Wow! You

really are an exceptionally brave man. Your family must be very proud!'

Returning the microphone to his mouth, she gave him a few moments *not* to tell her exactly how proud his family were of him, before bringing it back again to ask, 'And do you have any idea where Morose may be hiding out?'

He didn't, which wasn't surprising.

'Well, we won't take up any more of your time. Thank you again, Andrew. No doubt the residents of Portsmouth and beyond owe you a huge debt of gratitude, and I'm sure your family are very much looking forward to your safe return.'

Looking back at Will's iPhone, she signed off by saying, 'This is Abigail Love, for Hampshire Today, wishing Andrew Capstan a much deserved rest, and a speedy recovery. Back to the studio!'

Fixing a smile at Will's iPhone, she held it there for a few seconds, before letting out a relieved sigh.

'How was that?' she asked, as she turned around to the bedside table to open her handbag again, and shoved the microphone back in.

'Remarkably convincing,' replied Will, with unusual sincerity. 'Who's going to do the voice?'

'Our editor, Martin, normally does that sort of thing,' she answered. 'He's good at impersonations.'

As she leaned back over the patient to prise the sunglasses from his face, she said, 'Anyway, our work is done, and before that policeman outside comes in to find out what we've been up to, I suggest we get the hell out of here!'

CHAPTER SIX
A BODY AND A BEACH

BACK AT Hampshire Today's HQ, Eliot congratulated them both on their little coup, and Abigail only just had a chance to brief the news channel's Editor, Martin Grafham, on their need for a voiceover, and what sort of thing she thought Mr Inspector Capstan would have said during the relevant gaps in the dialogue, when a call came through saying that a body had been discovered, washed up on the beach, somewhere between Southsea Castle and South Parade Pier.

With a glimmer of hope that it might be the missing criminal mastermind, known simply as Morose, they set off once more, with Abigail back behind the wheel and Will sitting in the passenger seat, feeling a little more relaxed now, especially as the girl alongside him still seemed blissfully unaware of exactly who he was.

Picking up a couple of sandwiches and some coffee along the way, they parked up in the nearby *D-Day Museum* public car park and followed the path towards Southsea Castle and the southern coast of England beyond, tucking into their lunch as they went.

It wasn't long before they arrived at the steep stone steps that led down to the seafront about thirty feet below. From their vantage point they could see that a small crowd of about fifteen people had gathered around something near to where the waves were gently breaking below, but from where they were, they couldn't see what it was. It did look as if they'd managed to beat the Solent Police to it, which in fairness wasn't too difficult. They couldn't even see any competing news teams, who always had a tendency to stand out due to the enormous cameras they carted around with them. So, sensing another scoop, they trotted down the granite steps and marched their way over the shorefront towards the crowd.

As they drew near, Abigail pulled out her journalist's press pass from inside her handbag, a form of identity that always proved useful in such circumstances, and as she held it high, she called out, 'THERE'S NOTHING TO SEE HERE, PLEASE MOVE ON! MOVE ON PLEASE! NOTHING TO SEE!'

But there must have been something to see, or it was unlikely that they'd have all been there.

Assuming that the advancing couple were a plain-clothed police team, a crime scene investigation unit, Special Branch, MI5, Her Majesty's Coastguard, Import & Export officials, the Tax Evasion Police, or maybe even the Illegal Immigration Squad, the crowd turned back to take a few last selfies, spent a moment or two longer posting them up on to Facebook, and then slowly began to drift away.

As the crowd parted, Abigail and Will were given a clear, unobstructed view of what they'd all been gawping at; a giant headless body lying on its back wearing an ill-fitting dark blue suit, a badly stained office shirt, and a bedraggled stripy blue tie, all of which were accessorised by shiny clumps of dark green seaweed and about two dozen flies.

Will gagged at first sight. Despite having worked as a reporter for the Portsmouth Post for the last five years, he'd never seen a headless washed-up body before, and certainly not one within quite such close proximity.

Abigail's constitution, however, was a little more hardy, and waving the flies away, she crouched down to take a closer look.

Having spent a few moments examining the giant lump, she soon realised that he was missing a few other body parts as well.

'He doesn't have any hands, or feet!' she exclaimed over her shoulder to Will.

Will wasn't particularly interested. The missing head was bad enough, and it had already managed to put him off his half-eaten ham and cheese sandwich. So he discarded it over his shoulder and took a tentative sip from his coffee in a bid to settle his stomach and get rid of the taste of sick that had just arrived in his mouth.

Meanwhile, Abigail wasted little time in endeavouring to identify the body. *It has to be Morose*, she thought to herself. *It just has to be!*

Undoing the button that was only barely managing to hold the front of his suit jacket together, she eased her hand inside, searching for the pocket that was normally there, hoping to find some form of identification.

'What have we here?' she asked herself, and pulling out what turned out to be a soggy black leather wallet, she stood up to face Will as she opened it.

'Bingo!' she said, easing out a business card which

she held out in front of her, and with a triumphant smile, read out, 'Chief Inspector Morose, Solent Police!'

'You're kidding?'

'Nope! It's him alright! Now, come on, ditch that coffee and get your phone out. We've probably only got about five minutes before everyone else gets here.'

And with her dummy microphone retrieved from her handbag for the second time that day, Abigail did a quick hair and makeup check as Will set the two polystyrene coffee cups down onto the sand and pulled out his iPhone.

'You ready?' she asked.

'All set!' he answered.

'How do I look?'

Will shrugged. 'Better than that guy down there,' he said, nodding at the headless bloated corpse.

'No, seriously. Do I look OK?'

'You look fine.'

'Right!' And going through the same process as she'd done back at the hospital, shaking her hair out and licking her immaculate white teeth, she stared over at Will's iPhone.

'Is it on?' she asked.

'It's on,' he replied.

Taking a deep breath, she began, 'This is Abigail Love reporting from...oh, hold on. Where are we?'

'I'm not sure,' said Will, looking around. 'That's that castle thing over there, and that pier thing on that side, but I can't remember what they're called.'

'I'll just say we're on the beach. That will have to do. Are you ready?' she asked again.

'Yes, ready.'

'Is it still on?'

'It's on!'

'Are you sure?'

'Yes, of course I'm sure! Oh no, hang on. Sorry. It's on now.'

After giving Will a hard stare, she began again.

'This is Abigail Love reporting from a beach in Portsmouth. With us here today is none other than…no, scratch that. I'll have another go.'

Will thought it best not to express his feelings by telling her to hurry the fuck up, and simply continued to film.

'OK. Is it on?'

'Yes, it's on!' he said, mumbling *'for fuck's sake'* under his breath.

'Right.'

There was a momentary pause, before she started up again.

'This is Abigail Love reporting from Portsmouth's seafront, where lies the deformed, headless body of the man who went by the name of Morose, the former Chief Inspector of the Solent Police. As you're no doubt aware, this was the same man who was found guilty of multiple mass murders, and the one who, only last week, escaped from Portsmouth Prison, led a heavily armed group of insurgents over to the Isle of Wight, overthrew the newly established government and killed numerous innocent members of the local population in the process. And if it wasn't for our local hero, Inspector Andrew Capstan, he might still be there to this day. But as you can see…' and she stepped aside to allow Will to film the body, 'it looks like his bid to escape from the clutches of the law has left him like this: a washed-up, bloated old corpse, with neither head, hands nor feet to show for it.

'So, we can all sleep a little easier tonight, knowing that at least one dangerous nut-job is no more, and that justice has been done.

'This is Abigail Love, reporting for Hampshire Today. Back to the studio!'

As last time, she fixed a smile at Will's iPhone before letting out a heavy sigh and asking, 'How was that?'

Will couldn't help but be impressed. She clearly had a natural ability for public broadcasting, and she certainly looked good doing it. But it still didn't change the fact that this was the same girl who'd spent about five years at school calling him *Wee Willy Wankett*, before asking him if he'd managed to find his blankett, so he just said, 'It was all right,' and checked the video to make sure it had recorded properly.

'Gee, thanks,' said Abigail. Even Herman had been more supportive than that.

'What?' asked Will, and not willing to upset her too much, added, 'It was good. Here, take a look.'

Abigail joined him to watch the video playback. She was pleased. It *was* good, and she was now keen to get it to HQ where she was sure to have a little more of a positive response to what may have been her finest hour. With that in mind, she said, 'Come on then, let's get back!'

CHAPTER SEVEN
A CHANGE OF OWNERSHIP

ANCHORED ABOUT half a mile out from the same stretch of beach lay a 35-foot CloudCatcher sailing yacht. In the cockpit, behind the ship's wheel and gazing out towards the coastline through a pair of binoculars, stood another giant of a man, but this one with all his parts still very much attached; his head was bald, and his face featured a dark half-beard that had had the top lip shaved off.

It was Morose; the very man that Abigail and Will had thought they'd discovered, lying on the beach.

He'd been there for the last half hour or so observing the body's discovery with interest, because the yacht he was standing on wasn't his. It belonged to the other man, the one without a head.

It hadn't been his intention to steal a yacht, and certainly not to murder its owner. His original plan had begun the Friday before, when he'd "borrowed" a rowing boat to get him from the Isle of Wight over the Solent, back to his old home town of Portsmouth; but having found a suitable little boat moored up in Fishbourne Harbour, after only about five minutes of rowing he'd realised that he was never going to make it. He was, after all, enormous, and his body weight alone was making the job nigh-on impossible.

So he'd headed for the nearest decent-sized yacht, one that could support his vast physical mass.

It had been remarkably easy to steal it, but less so to

dispose of its owner. Having heaved himself aboard, he was about to start the engine, something that wasn't too difficult to do as the keys were already in the ignition, when the owner had stumbled out into the cockpit, half-asleep, wearing his pyjamas. He must have heard Morose's rowing boat bump against the hull and had dragged himself out to investigate. But he'd probably have stayed locked in the cabin below with a flare gun pointed at the door had he known that the thing that bumped the side was a boat helmed by the infamous escaped convict Morose, the former Chief Inspector of the Solent Police, otherwise known as the Psychotic Serial Slasher of Southampton and the South Coast, on the run after his failed invasion of the Isle of Wight.

Seeing the bleary-eyed owner emerge from below deck, Morose had little choice but to retrieve the boat hook that he'd used to help climb aboard to put a sizeable dent in the owner's head, one deep enough to kill him on impact.

And as the boat hook struck the man, an idea hit Morose that made him think Lady Luck must have been smiling down on him, and it was about time too, as she'd been remarkably absent for the last couple of years.

The man he'd just taken care of, the assumed legal owner of the yacht, just happened to be similar in both shape and size to him; in other words, he was really fat, and must have weighed well-over two hundred kilograms, easy! The physical likeness had provided Morose with a brand new plan, something he'd been lacking since finding himself cornered on top of Ryde

Town Hall's roof, back on the Isle of Wight. His new idea wasn't complicated, and was hardly revolutionary. It was simply to fake his own death for the chance to begin again, with a clean slate, so to speak.

Leaving the wooden rowing boat behind, as his new yacht had a decent-sized tender with an outboard engine, he'd motored out into the Solent to spend a relaxing weekend recuperating and thinking more about his new scheme, the first part of which was to make everyone think that he was Morose no more.

It was with that in mind that he'd exchanged clothes with the yacht's previous owner, making sure to leave his wallet, which he'd retrieved from his personal effects before escaping from Portsmouth Prison, inside his suit jacket pocket . He'd then used an old trick he'd developed back in the day as a Police Chief Inspector, the one he'd devised when he'd needed a few unidentifiable bodies to help boost his police quarterly bonus.

And so, long before the sun rose on Monday morning, he'd taken the six inch sailing knife that was kept sheathed beside the ship's wheel and which was designed to saw through rope, and busied himself with the somewhat irksome task of removing the former owner's head, hands and feet, so making physical identification considerably more challenging. The bits he'd didn't need he'd discarded casually over the yacht's side, knowing that the local marine life would make short work of them. The body itself he'd dragged down onto the bathing platform at the boat's stern, and into the tender. He'd then motored the tender and the body into shore, moored up on the sand, rolled the former boat's owner off, and headed back to his yacht, very much looking forward to getting his new life underway.

When he'd observed the official looking couple approach the discarded body, wave off the crowd and discover his wallet, he'd felt confident that his plan had been a success. Knowing the Solent Police as he did, he felt it was unlikely they'd bother to go to the expense of running a full DNA check. People generally saw what they wanted to see, and he had little doubt that the local authorities, as well as the national press, were especially keen for him to turn up somewhere dead.

With a broad fat grin, he brought his binoculars down, squeezed himself around the ship's wheel, and made his way into the cabin to shave off his beard, the first item on the list for a change of identity. He'd then have to look around for some paint, as his second job was to give his yacht a new name. It was currently called *Windy Bottom*, which was just embarrassing. It was also likely that at some point either a friend or family member would report the recently deceased as being missing, at which time the coastguard would be keeping an eye out for it. He wasn't too worried though. There must have been hundreds of 35-foot CloudCatcher yachts dotted in and around the Solent area. Even if he didn't change the name, as long as he stayed away from the marinas, it would be difficult to find him. However, once he had re-christened it, he knew with absolute certainty that he'd become virtually invisible.

CHAPTER EIGHT
MATCHMAKING

ARRIVING BACK at Hampshire Today's HQ, Abigail and Will made their way straight over to Eliot's office. A quick glance through his partition window revealed that he was in a meeting with their editor, Martin Grafham, but knowing the importance of the video they had, she gave the door a tentative knock, pushed it open and poked her head inside.

'Sorry to bother you,' she said, 'but I have news from that body, down on the beach.'

Eliot sent her a look of hopeful expectation. 'I don't suppose there was any chance it was Morose?'

A huge smile spread over her face.

'It was!' she announced. 'And not only that, but we were first on site *and* we managed to make another exclusive video!'

Eliot leapt up from his chair, and with an excited grin headed around his desk towards her, extending his hand as he did.

'Fantastic, Abigail! Good work! Just brilliant!'

Martin stood to offer his own congratulations. 'You've certainly had quite a day of it, haven't you?' he said, taking his turn to shake her hand.

Feeling unusually modest, Abigail said, 'It helped having a decent cameraman, for a change,' and glanced over her shoulder at Will, who was lurking somewhat awkwardly, just outside the office door.

'Yes, of course,' said Eliot. 'Come in, Will - don't be

shy.'

Whenever Will was told not to be shy, it generally had the opposite effect, and still lacking confidence in this brand new working environment, especially as he wasn't sure he even had a job there yet, he slunk in with an apprehensive look. 'What should I do with the video?' he asked, holding out his iPhone in a bid to deflect attention away from himself.

Martin spoke up.

'Let's have a quick look at it now, then we can see if it needs work before uploading to our YouTube channel.'

Will found the relevant file, opened it up, touched the play icon and held it out for Eliot and Martin to watch.

A couple of minutes later, Eliot turned to face Abigail. 'You know, I think that's your finest work to date, don't you?'

'Possibly,' she said, and for modesty's sake, added, 'It took a couple of takes though.'

'And the body was definitely that of Morose?'

'Well, as you saw in the video, it didn't come with a head, so we weren't sure at first, but then we found his wallet, inside his suit jacket pocket, and as it's not every day that a body turns up around here, especially not quite such a large one, I can't imagine who else it could have been.'

'No, fair enough,' said Elliot, who had no desire for it to be anyone other than the Psychotic Serial Slasher of Southampton and the South Coast. 'Martin, you'd better get that video uploaded onto our YouTube channel, pronto!'

'Roger that,' answered Martin, before asking Will, 'If I could borrow your phone?'

'Oh, yes, of course,' he replied. 'Here you are,' and he handed it over.

'Thanks! I'll just upload the video and then bring it straight back.'

Martin made his way past Abigail and Will and out of the door as Eliot returned to his desk.

'You two seem to be working rather well together,' observed Eliot, as he sat back in his chair. 'Are you OK to keep things as they are for a while?'

They both shrugged, neither looking as if they were willing to commit, so Eliot directed his attention at Will and rephrased the question. 'Are you happy to keep working as Abigail's cameraman?'

Will turned to give Abigail the briefest of glances. If he'd been asked that question when he'd first seen her, at the beginning of the day, it would have been a no-brainer. But now that he knew exactly who she was, he found himself torn between two distinct sides of his personality. The one that kept him safe, and protected his psychological well-being from harm, wanted to get just as far away from Fanny-Gail the Horrible as possible. Yes, she didn't know who he was yet, but if he took the job she was going to find out; maybe not that day, or the next, but at some point she'd definitely discover that he was the boy she'd spent five years calling Wee Willy Wankett, the one who seemed to have permanently lost his blankett. And when she did, it would be Whitworth School all over again!

However, looking at the girl from a purely hedonistic perspective, Abigail Love was most definitely his type. There was no doubt about that. In fairness, she was probably everyone's type - men, women, gay or straight - and he'd fallen for her the moment she'd walked into the office. So, although he thought he had a choice to make, that of either walking away to probably end up being forced to move back in with his mum, or taking the job and risk having to re-live his secondary school days, there was really only one option available to him. After all, he was single, he hadn't had sex in more months than he cared to count, and she was by far the most attractive girl he'd met in a very long time.

'Oh, er, well, it's OK, I suppose,' he replied, but as he was still a little upset that it wasn't the job he'd come for, asked, 'but I was really hoping to work as a news correspondent.'

'Look,' said Eliot, as he leaned back in his chair, 'you two clearly work well together. If Abigail's happy, maybe she could mentor you while you continue to work as her cameraman? And then, after a few months or so, depending on how you get on, we could possibly promote you?'

Will still didn't seem to be champing at the bit as Eliot would have expected. After all, he was offering him the chance to hang out with an absolute stunner, and get paid too. So he looked over at Abigail and asked, 'What do you think?'

'I'd be OK with that,' she said, giving Will what could have been considered an encouraging smile.

Naturally she was secretly thrilled by the idea. Not only did he smell of something other than urine and alcohol, he was about three thousand times better looking than her previous cameraman, and could even qualify as being one of the most attractive men currently on the Portsmouth market, which wasn't saying much, but it was something at least. Having already planned how they were going to live out the rest of their lives together, she'd spent the latter part of the day trying to work out how she could ask him out, and in such a way as to make him think that she hadn't.

'So, it's agreed then?' asked Eliot, looking at Will and thinking that the boy would have to be either completely stupid or extraordinarily gay to say anything other than yes.

After another brief pause, Will eventually said, 'All right, I'll do it!'

Eliot let out a sigh of relief. For a moment there he was honestly beginning to think the boy was going to say no.

'Good job,' he said, and glanced down at his watch. 'Well, look, it's just gone four. Why don't you both head off a little early and get yourselves a drink somewhere. You've had a great day, and you deserve some sort of a celebration!'

Realising that her boss had just set them up on a date, Abigail thought to herself, *That was easy!*

But now that she was actually about to go out with him, she suddenly felt rather nervous. So she asked Eliot, 'Can't you join us?'

'Unfortunately not,' he answered. He'd no intention of getting in the way of what he hoped would be the beginning of a highly profitable office romance, at least not until he'd had a chance to discuss the subject of Will's salary with him. No doubt the boy would be more amenable to taking the sort of thing he was thinking of offering, which wasn't much, if they were hooked up together. 'You two head off, and have a great time. And I'll see you both back here for the production meeting tomorrow morning.'

CHAPTER NINE
CRIMEWATCH UK

SOON AFTER Abigail and Will left, Martin came back to Eliot's office, having returned Will's iPhone to him.

'Those two seem to be working well together,' he said, as he closed the door behind him.

'Yes, and I'm encouraging it, for now,' said Eliot. 'How about a drink?' Without waiting for an answer, he pulled open the bottom drawer of his desk where he kept a bottle of twelve year old Glenfiddich whisky and a couple of tumblers.

'And I thought landing both the Capstan and Morose stories was a bit of a coup!' added Martin, as he re-took his seat.

Eliot passed a glass over to his editor and leaned back in his chair. 'It was,' he answered, as he swirled his drink around before knocking the whole thing back. Catching his breath, he went on, 'but it presents us with a bit of a problem.'

'How do you mean?' Martin also finished the contents of his glass in one gulp and returned it to the desk for a refill.

'We've been living off Morose for months now,' he said, as he poured out two more glasses. 'If it wasn't for him turning from Police Chief Inspector, to mass murderer, to escaped convict, to criminal mastermind, to invading insurgent, I doubt we'd have had the success we've had so far. And without him being around anymore, I'm really not sure how we're going to survive.'

'I see your point,' Martin nodded, taking the refreshed glass, knocking it back and returning it to the desk.

'And if we realistically ever want to graduate from the two-hour live YouTube broadcaster we are now, to the pioneering twenty-four hour news channel as per the original plan, we're going to have to find a hell of lot more to talk about other than the weather!'

With that he too downed his glass and re-filled both tumblers.

'It's only then that we'll be able to get these viewing figures up,' he continued, reaching for the latest audience report that they'd been discussing before Abigail and Will had come in. 'And until we do that, we're never going to be able to attract the sort of high calibre advertisers we need.'

They took a moment to ponder the problem as they each took a more moderate sip from their drinks.

'How about we start doing some more feature news items?' Martin suggested.

'What did you have in mind?'

'Well, the BBC has *Newsnight* and *Question Time*, which are basically just extensions of the news. They've also got *The One Show*, which is people chatting about the news. Then there's *Have I Got News for You?* which is people making fun of the news, and then there's *Crimewatch* of course, which is just the news, all over again. Couldn't we start doing something like those?'

'I suspect we'd have budget issues,' mused Eliot,

'and I can't imagine a version of *Crimewatch* working around here. Before Morose came on the scene, nothing seemed to happen, ever!'

It was true. Hampshire had historically always been a quiet county, but knowing that, as Eliot must have done, as he'd been brought up in Southampton, Martin couldn't help but wonder why he'd decided to set up a news channel based in Portsmouth, and not in a location with a little more chance of some action, like Glasgow, or Birmingham. Even somewhere like Morden would have probably been a safer bet. Not that Martin minded. It had given him a job, which he'd been struggling to find before, and remembering that, and sensing that his property investor turned wannabe media tycoon boss seemed to be a little down, he continued to try to offer some encouraging remarks.

'We still get the occasional fight outside a night club.'

'True,' said Eliot, as he stared up at the ceiling. 'I suppose we could set up some hidden cameras in front of all the main ones and just report on what happens.' He took another sip from his drink. 'But that would only work if we could afford to keep broadcasting through the night.'

'Maybe we could just film outside the clubs and then report on what happened the next day?'

'I suppose. But it would be far better if we could run live commentary off it.'

'Why don't we just film a roundabout?' suggested Martin.

'Sorry, I'm not with you.'

'If we stick a hidden camera on, say, the Marketway

Roundabout, near Safebusy's, we could just run commentary off that!'

'Why? Is it particularly busy around there?'

'It is when I have to drive around it on the way here, and there's always some muppet-brained moron doing something stupid. We could set up a few of them around all the black-spots in Portsmouth and call it *Trafficwatch*!'

'OK, well, it's not a bad idea,' said Eliot, and surprisingly it wasn't.

'And what about all those missing pets we've had recently?' Martin was clearly on a roll. 'Couldn't we start a *Crimewatch* type thing, but call it *Petwatch* instead? Then we could show loads of pictures of missing animals and ask people to phone in if they've seen them.'

Eliot imagined someone wearing glasses with a serious, intense look about them, staring at the camera and asking, 'Have you seen this dog?'

'Do you really think anyone would be interested?' he asked, unconvinced.

'I think you'd be surprised how much people like looking at pictures of other people's pets,' replied Martin, who just happened to have two dogs, three cats, five budgerigars, a gerbil, and a hedgehog who popped by occasionally. He also had a digital SLR camera and an Instagram account, and loved nothing more than taking pictures of them all. 'And I'd have thought it would be a relatively straight forward job to find a sponsor.'

'It's not a bad idea,' said Eliot, 'I suppose,' and he leaned forward to put his drink down so that he could take some notes.

'Is there anything coming up in the diary?' asked Martin, still trying to be helpful.

'Not a huge amount.' Eliot pulled his laptop towards him so that he could open up their shared Google calendar. 'All the main summer events are over, and there's nothing much else going on until Trafalgar Day on the 21st October. Last year I remember they fired off some of HMS Victory's cannons, so it's worth covering, just in case one of them's been loaded by accident and takes out some Sea Cadets. But there's not much we can really rely on with any certainty until Bonfire Night, when there's always some idiot who manages to set fire to themselves. Looking ahead after that, the next big event's not until the Southampton Boat Show in January.'

'What about Halloween?'

'Well, yes. A trick-or-treater may take things a little too far with a kitchen knife, so again we'd need to keep an eye on it.'

'Isn't the UKIP Conference starting tomorrow?'

'At the Grande Escargot Hotel in town, but it's a non-event. I was down there last year and you wouldn't have even known it was going on.'

'But it's different this year, surely?' asked Martin.

'What, you mean because of Brexit?'

'That, and the US Election, yes.'

'Really?' asked Eliot, who considered the idea of covering an unelectable party's conference to be about as dull as your average energy efficient lightbulb.

But Martin felt they should do something, or else

they could end up sitting there all night, drinking to a point beyond depression that could easily see them deciding to close the company down before taking it in turns to jump out of the window.

'Why don't we head down there now and take a look?'

'Have they got a bar?' asked Eliot, who was already enjoying the effects of the two and a half glasses of whisky he'd so far consumed, and was subsequently keen for a few more.

'Oh, I'm sure they do. C'mon. It's only down the road, and the walk will do us good.'

CHAPTER TEN
I PREDICT A RIOT

THEY STROLLED along Millennium Walkway from their office just off Gunwharf Road, heading towards the vibrant complex that surrounded Spinnaker Tower, where the Grande Escargot Hotel was located.

Crossing the small stretch of water towards the Old Custom House pub, they could hear some sort of commotion over towards the nearby quayside. As they rounded the next corner, it turned out that Martin was right after all; there actually *was* something going on.

Lining the steep stone steps that led up to the hotel were a huge number of protestors, waving an assortment of placards as they chanted, *'UKIP NO, WE REALLY DON'T THINK SO!'* in perfect unison. The number of them was so great, that even the Solent Police had been called, and they'd formed a human barricade around the hotel's frontage in what looked like an attempt to keep the disgruntled mob from burning the place to the ground. Although they didn't have any riot gear on, they did all have their truncheons out, and were waggling them at the protestors in a highly provocative manner.

Seeing the commotion, Eliot stopped dead in his tracks and pulled out his phone.

'We need to get someone down here to cover this,' he said to Martin, as he started to dial. 'I'll try Abigail. She might be nearby.'

Indeed she was - just down the road in the Badger & Hamster pub, with Will. As it was only about a ten minute walk away, Eliot asked her if they wouldn't mind popping down, promising them a drink or two if they did.

Ending the call, Eliot said, 'She said she'd come. Let's go and see if there's anything going on inside.'

Pushing and shoving through the seething mass of protestors, Eliot and Martin eventually managed to make their way up the stone steps where they were met by the line of police, who all looked more than a little agitated.

As the demonstrators surrounding them continued to chant, *UKIP NO, WE REALLY DON'T THINK SO!'* Eliot called over to the nearest policeman, 'IS IT OK IF WE GO IN?'

'UKIP PARTY MEMBERS ONLY TODAY. SORRY!' shouted the police constable in return, trying to be heard over the protestors' cry, *UKIP NO, WE REALLY DON'T THINK SO!'*

'WE'RE FROM UKIP,' Eliot replied. 'WE JUST LEFT OUR ROSETTES INSIDE THE HOTEL.'

UKIP NO, WE REALLY DON'T THINK SO!'

'WHAT, BOTH OF YOU?' asked the policeman, as he stared at them with clear suspicion.

UKIP NO, WE REALLY DON'T THINK SO!'

'YES. ME AND HIM!' Eliot said, pointing a thumb at Martin.

UKIP NO, WE REALLY DON'T THINK SO!'

They looked the part, being that they were white, and were smartly dressed in suits and ties, so the officer said, 'GO ON THEN, BUT I WOULDN'T

BE IN A HURRY TO COME OUT AGAIN IF I WERE YOU!'

'UKIP NO, WE REALLY DON'T THINK SO!'

'UNDERSTOOD!' he called back, and as the crowd continued to chant, *'UKIP NO, WE REALLY DON'T THINK SO!'* the policeman stepped aside to allow them through.

Inside the hotel the atmosphere couldn't have been more different. Yes, it was equally as busy, and it was almost as loud, but the dozens of guests milling about in the lobby, and over towards the bar, all wearing their highly distinctive purple and yellow UKIP rosettes, seemed to be full of good humour and Party cheer.

After weaving their way to the bar, Eliot raised his voice to ask Martin, 'What are you having?' as he retrieved his wallet from his inside suit jacket pocket.

'A pint of Portsmouth Pride, please.'

Catching the eye of the nearest bartender, and holding out a twenty-pound note, Eliot called out, 'Two pints of Portsmouth Pride, please?'

As they waited patiently for their drinks, they took the opportunity to have a look around, trying to spot any well-known personalities, like the party's leader, Mr Michael Suntage, for example. Eliot collected his change, and they pushed their way through the throng towards one of the bay windows where they'd spotted a couple of high round bar tables, one of which was free.

Eliot heaved his padded black laptop bag onto the table so that he could keep an eye on it. 'I didn't know

UKIP was so popular,' he said as loudly as he could without actually shouting.

'I think it's the whole referendum thing,' replied Martin, with equal volume. 'It seems to have brought a lot of them out of the closet.'

'But this place is heaving! When I was here last year, there was only a couple of old men and a dog.'

'Oh, really?' said Martin, with interest. 'What sort was it?'

Eliot cupped his ear and asked, 'Say again?'

'I asked, what sort was it?'

'What sort of what was it?'

'The dog. The one that was here last year?'

Giving his editor a funny sort of a look, Eliot said. 'I've really no idea. I just remember that there was one.'

'Yes, but which type?'

'That's just what I said. I don't know. I'm not really a dog sort of a person.'

With a confused look, Martin asked, 'You don't like dogs?' as if the man had just said that he didn't like football.

'I didn't say that. I just said that I'm not really a dog sort of a person.'

Martin couldn't believe that it was possible for someone *not* to be a dog sort of a person, and so assuming that it must have been a certain breed he wasn't keen on, asked, 'So which ones don't you like, then?'

'I really don't know,' replied Eliot, wishing that he'd never brought the subject up. 'To be honest,' he continued, 'they all look the same to me.'

Now he'd managed to offend his editor.

'What do you mean, they all look the same? How can they possibly all look the same?'

Backpedalling, Eliot said, 'You know. They've all got four legs, two ears and a tail.'

'And you don't like any of them?'

'Well, the medium-sized ones are all right, I suppose.'

'How about Belgian Tervurens?'

'I thought they were chocolates?' asked Elliot, in an effort to lighten the mood a little.

'Of course they're not!' exclaimed Martin, unable to see how a Belgium Tervuren dog could possibly be compared to a chocolate. With that in mind, he began to describe to Eliot exactly what that specific breed of dog was like. 'A Belgian Tervuren is a herding dog with a dark brown coat and a black overlay. They're a bit like a German Shephard, just smaller, but they make particularly good pets and are very obedient. However, they do need plenty of exercise and mental stimulation.'

'Jesus, Martin! I'd no idea you liked dogs so much!'

'No more than most!' he answered, in a defensive tone.

But it wasn't true. Martin knew that he had what some would consider to be an unnatural interest in them. However, in his defence, he liked all animals, apart from goats, which he thought had weird eyes. But dogs were great, and he couldn't think of any reason for someone not to like them.

An awkward silence followed.

Rather keen not to fall out with his editor of several

months now, and who he was beginning to think of as more of a friend than an employee, Elliot decided to force a change of subject.

Gazing absently around, he said, 'It really is packed in here,' and then thought to add, 'Imagine if there was a bomb! Like that one back in the eighties, in Brighton.'

A middle-aged lady standing opposite gave him an odd look.

'It would certainly solve a few of our editorial problems,' said Martin, in an agreeable tone. He too was keen to clear the air between them and get back to discussing something more work related. 'Although,' he continued, 'not when we're standing right next to it,' and looked meaningfully down at Eliot's lap top bag with a mischievous grin.

Having exchanged smiles they both felt much better about each other, but out of the corner of his eye, Eliot noticed the same middle-aged lady whispering into the ear of the man beside her as she half-pointed at Eliot's padded laptop bag.

'A bomb?' the man asked, with a look of astonishment, and certainly with enough volume for those around him to hear.

Sensing a possible awkward situation developing, Eliot looked at the couple and with his most charming smile, said, 'It's not a bomb. We were joking. It's just my laptop.'

The dozen or so people who were standing around them all stopped talking, and began to slowly edge backwards, away from what did look very much like a suspicious object that could easily contain five kilos of plastic explosives and a digital alarm clock.

'Honestly, it was a joke,' said Eliot again, and keen to alleviate the fears of those still edging away, added, 'It really is just my laptop,' and went to pick it up.

The lady who'd first observed the package dropped her glass and let out a terror-inducing scream, as she grabbed hold of the man next to her.

Equally convinced, the man pointed at the case and shouted, 'EVERYONE OUT, THERE'S A BOMB!'

A wave of panic swept the bar area, spilled out into the lobby, leaked through to the kitchen, into the women's toilets, then the men's, then the disabled next door, and finally up the stairs, taking one floor at a time. As the rallying cry, 'EVERYONE OUT, THERE'S A BOMB!' was picked up by every man, woman, and cleaner, the entire hotel population ran screaming for the nearest and most obvious exit point, being the one at the front.

'We'd better make ourselves scarce,' said Eliot to Martin, as he downed his drink with one hand and grabbed his laptop bag with the other.

'You could be right there,' agreed Martin, who also finished off his pint and joined Eliot and the hundred or so others to form what could be described as a tidal wave of humanity, albeit a small one, surging towards the double doors that made up the hotel's entrance.

CHAPTER ELEVEN
A GOOD CHANCE OF A BONUS

BEFORE TAKING Eliot's call, what was effectively a date for Abigail and Will had been going as well as could be expected for a first one, and both were more nervous than they would have liked. Subsequently, small talk had dominated their walk down to the Badger & Hamster pub that stood opposite HMS Victory, the ship made famous by Lord Nelson at the Battle of Trafalgar in 1805, and by Cate Jakebury, otherwise known as Cut-Throat Cate, two years previously.

'Do you have any brothers and sisters?' was one of the questions they'd asked each other, and 'What sort of music do you like? Do you like reading? What's your favourite book? What's your favourite film? What star sign are you? Do you have any pets? What are their names? What colour are they?' and so forth, in the age-old game of feigning enough interest in someone so that they'll have sex with you.

But once they reached the pub and downed their first three drinks in quick succession, the conversation became less vacuous, and they moved onto more interesting subjects, which was how they discovered mutual agreement regarding their stance on leaving the European Union, and the US election.

They'd just managed to move the conversation on to the matter of Morose's widely reported fall from grace, when Abigail's phone rang.

Seeing that it was her boss, she popped outside the pub to take the call. On her return she smiled at Will. 'There's a protest going on outside the Grande Escargot Hotel, just down the road. Eliot wants us to cover it.'

'What, now?' asked Will, who up until that moment had been making good inroads into Abigail's pants, or at least he thought he had.

'He said he'd buy us a round if we do, and it's not every day we get a demonstration to report on. You never know, it could turn ugly!'

'And that's a reason to go?'

'You've got a lot to learn about television journalism, young Will…er? You know something, I don't know what your surname is.'

But that was a conversation Will definitely did *not* want to have, so he downed his drink, glanced at his watch and said, 'We'd better be on our way then. I'd hate to miss the story.'

Delighted to see him show a spark of enthusiasm for the job, she winked at him, took hold of his hand and said, 'C'mon then! It should be fun!'

Will couldn't see what could possibly be fun about covering a demonstration, especially as historically such things did seem to have a tendency to become violent, but the wink alone was enough to convince him to go, and he was more than happy for her to lead him out of the pub towards the Grande Escargot Hotel.

Rounding the same corner that Eliot and Martin had circumnavigated only about half an hour earlier, they saw that things were certainly heating up. There were hundreds of protestors, most of whom appeared to have brought placards, and they all seemed to be chanting the same message in perfect unison.

With her heart pounding with excitement, Abigail turned to Will and said, 'Are you ready to go again?'

Will couldn't remember going the first time; but then he realised that she was referring to his role as her cameraman, and dug out his iPhone for the third shoot of the day.

Abigail pulled her microphone out from her handbag, gave her hair a quick prod and was about to check her makeup when she thought, *Sod it*, and asked Will, 'Do I look all right?'

Will spent a moment framing her so that the hotel could be seen in the background, along with the police and a fair few of the protestors, and feeling more upbeat about where their relationship seemed to be going, called out, 'You look great!'

She returned a beaming smile, shook her hair out, licked her teeth and asked, 'Is it on?'

'It's on.'

'Are you sure?'

Double checking to make sure that it was this time, Will answered, 'Yes, it's definitely on.'

'OK,' she said, and look briefly at the scene behind, taking a moment to think about how she was going to start. Then she turned back to Will's iPhone, and began.

'This is Abigail Love reporting from outside the Grande Escargot Hotel in Portsmouth, where a large crowd has gathered to protest the UKIP Party

Conference that is due to start here tomorrow. Let's see if we can have a word with one of the protestors.'

Turning to approach towards the crowd, she picked out a large man holding a placard high above his head, and yelling with rabid fury, 'UKIP NO, WE REALLY DON'T THINK SO!'

'Excuse me?' she asked, tugging on the protestor's coat.

Stopping mid chant, the well-built man, who had a shaved head, a crooked jaw and a broken nose, scowled down at her.

'I'm reporting from Hampshire Today. Can you tell me why you're here?' She held out her microphone for his answer.

'Oh, yes, of course. I'm here as part of the protest.'

'So it would appear, but what is it that you're protesting against?'

'Oh, well, it's um…UKIP no, we really don't think so, isn't it?' answered the man, but without much confidence.

'We can hear that. But what is it about UKIP that you don't like, exactly?'

'Ah yes,' and he pulled down his banner to read it for the lady. 'UKIP'S SHIT!' he said. 'That's what my sign says, anyway.'

'I see,' said Abigail. 'And in what way?'

'Um…I'm not sure, really.'

'But you must have an opinion why you think UKIP is, er, not very good?'

'Well, to be honest,' he said, looking over both shoulders, 'I think they're all right. I even voted for them at the last election.'

Abigail glanced over at Will with a questioning look, but he just shrugged back at her.

'So why are you here then?' she asked, looking back up at the man.

'It's my job. I work for WeProtestAnyDomonstration.com. Well, part-time at least.'

Abigail sighed. She'd heard about professional protestors before, but up until that moment had thought they were an urban myth, used to take the blame by whichever person or organisation it was that was being protested against.

But realising she may have just stumbled onto a story within a story, she said, 'That's interesting. And what does the job involve?'

'It's simple really. I just show up at wherever the protest is supposed to take place, someone gives me a placard and tells me what to shout. That's it really.'

'And does it pay well?'

'It's all right, I guess. But we get more if there's a fight.'

'Why's that?' asked Abigail. 'Are you not insured?'

'Oh no, nothing like that. It's just that they give us a bonus if we're able to start one.'

'I see. And how many of the people here would you say were being paid to be here?'

'Oh, er, well. All of us, I think! Although I did meet an old lady earlier who said she was a volunteer.'

'And what would you say makes for a good professional protester?'

'Um...' said the man, as he gazed up at the grey autumnal sky. 'I've never thought about it really. I suppose you'd have to like shouting a lot, and getting involved in fights. But most of us are unemployed football supporters, so that sort of stuff kind of comes naturally.'

'And which football team do you support?'

'Arsenal. Sometimes Chelsea. It depends whose playing. Anyway, I'd better get back to work now, before my line manager sees me talking,' and with that he turned round, held up his banner again and picked up where he'd left off, shouting, 'UKIP NO, WE REALLY DON'T THINK SO!' with exactly the same intense angry conviction that he'd had before taking part in the interview.

Abigail looked back at Will's phone, saying, 'Let's see if we can talk to someone else.'

Just as she said that, screams were heard drifting down from the hotel, and looking up, Abigail saw UKIP party members spewing out of the entrance and slamming straight into the surrounding policemen.

Sensing an opportunity for a bonus, the mob of protestors surged forward to meet their quarry, leaving the Solent Police sandwiched between them and the UKIP delegates, one side seemingly desperate to vacate the hotel, and the other rather keen to earn some extra money.

As Abigail watched, and Will filmed, they soon saw the thin blue line of police disappear as a massive fist fight broke out between the two opposing forces.

'Er…' said Abigail, as she looked back at Will's iPhone, unsure as to what to say, but she soon found the right words. 'It seems that, for some unknown reason, the UKIP delegates have decided to leave the

Grande Escargot Hotel and mount what does appear to be an all-out assault against the protestors. We're not exactly sure why they've done this, but maybe the constant chanting and abuse all became too much for them. Let's go and see if we can have a word with some of them.'

Will looked up at her and shook his head in a bid to discourage such an idea. Even after she'd beckoned him to follow, he continued to hold his ground. It was only when she said, '*Come on!*' to him through gritted teeth that he reluctantly followed on after.

They made their way up the stone steps towards the hotel's entrance, where it was fairly obvious that the professional protestors, with their natural temperament for violence and years of training as British Football Supporters, had the upper hand. But after just a few minutes the tide seemed to be turning, as some of the larger and more passionate of UKIP's party members made the most of the opportunity to take out some of their pent-up aggression against those who were opposed to their way of thinking.

With a stroke of luck, Abigail spotted UKIP's Party Leader, Michael Suntage, locked in what looked like some sort of wrestling bout with a protestor of similar size and weight.

'Mr Suntage! Mr Suntage!' she called. 'May we have a few words?'

'What, now?' asked the UKIP Party Leader, busy trying to hook his fingers into his opponent's nostrils.

'Just a few quick questions?' she prompted, as she watched them rotate in front of her.

'Can't we do it another time?'

'Not really, no,' said Abigail.

'Oh, for fuck's sake! Go on then, but make it quick!'

'Mr Suntage. Why was it that you decided to launch an unprovoked attack on what was nothing more than a peaceful demonstration?'

'We didn't!'

'Well, that's how it looked from where I was standing.'

'Listen, Miss—?'

'Love. Abigail Love, from Hampshire Today.'

'Listen, Miss Love, I've no idea where you were standing or what you saw, but from my Party's perspective we had no choice. Some immigrant bastard planted a bomb in the hotel, so it was either stay there and get blown up, or come out here and take a beating! Now if you don't mind, I do seem to have my hands full at the moment. Ow…fuck! Those are my testicles, you immigrant-loving bastard!' With that, Mr Suntage gave up trying to hook his fingers into his opponent's nostrils, and jammed them into his eyes instead.

'AAAAARRRRRGGGGGGGHHHHHHH!' screamed the protestor, and they both fell over on the steps and began rolling down to the bottom, continuing their no-holds barred wrestling contest as they went.

With a serious look, Abigail turned back to the camera. 'So there you have it: UKIP's Party Leader, Mr Michael Suntage, blaming a bomb inside the hotel as the reason for launching an unprovoked attack on an innocent group of protestors. But as we can clearly see, the hotel behind me is still very much intact, unlike the vast majority of his party members, which must be final proof that Michael Suntage is a lying sack of shit after all. This is Abigail Love, reporting from outside the Grande Escargot Hotel in Portsmouth.'

CHAPTER TWELVE
HOW TO MAKE A
CHARITABLE WITHDRAWAL

WATCHING THE UKIP demonstration from the side lines, or at least the coffee shop next door to the Grande Escargot Hotel, was none other than Morose.

Having spent the afternoon shopping in Portsmouth, he'd wandered down to the shorefront near Spinnaker Tower to buy a local paper, and find a suitable cafe from where he'd be able to gaze out at his new yacht, anchored about half a mile from the coast.

His shopping trip had been a huge success, by a man's standards at any rate, as he'd been able to pick up everything he'd needed with a speed that could easily have set a new world record, had anyone been timing him. Items purchased included a new suit, a fine selection of ties, a pair of jeans, a few polo shirts, a couple of jumpers, a pair of black office shoes, and some trainers. He'd also picked up a waterproof coat, some sunglasses, and a trendy dark grey flat cap, and had managed to find them all from just one department store, the Marks & Spencer on the high street.

He'd decided to buy himself a complete new wardrobe for two reasons, the first being that he really didn't like the garments that his recently deceased benefactor had left for him. As it turned out, the yacht's previous owner, who's headless body was in the process of being scooped up off the beach by a mini-digger, had the most appalling taste in clothes. From the look of them, he must have spent far more time living in the Caribbean than off the coast of Southern England, as his entire collection looked like they'd been designed by Laura Ashley during an LSD-inspired camping trip to the Glastonbury Festival.

The second reason was because of what he'd been up to earlier, which was making some rather hasty cash withdrawals from the charity shops that were so numerous in Portsmouth that they out-numbered estate agents by five to one. He'd been forced to do this because the said recently deceased benefactor, although evidently quite well-off, had only a £20 note and some loose change on him at the time of his death. He had the usual array of credit cards jammed into his wallet, but Morose had no idea what the associated pin numbers were, and had never been one for online shopping. Besides, for Morose's initial plans to come to fruition, what he needed was cash, and a fair amount of it. He'd focused on charity shops because he'd learnt, during his many years as the Chief Inspector of the Solent Police, that they always made the easiest target. To successfully rob one, all you had to do was pick a particularly hard-to-reach item displayed in the front window, walk in, and ask the old lady behind the counter if she'd be kind enough to fetch it for a closer look. While she risked a cardiac arrest in the name of Blind Dogs for the Guides, or whatever the charity was called, to retrieve the item in question, the thieving miscreant would simply reach over the counter, open the till and remove its contents. As long as the thief was able to maintain a conversation with the lady about how much the world had changed since the invention of the printing press, it would work every time.

It was, however, more complicated if there happened to be two old ladies perched behind the counter, but was still a fairly straight forward process. Whilst one would be weaving her way to the front of the shop, the expectant thief just needed to send the other in the opposite direction, towards the back, asking if a particular book that just happened to be at the very end of the highest shelf in the shop would make a suitable birthday present for a three year old. By the time they'd managed to retrieve the items, the robber would have vanished, along with the cash, leaving the old ladies wondering if he, or she, had ever been there in the first place. Furthermore, they often didn't even realise that they'd been robbed until the shop closed and they started to cash up. But even then, most wouldn't report it, as they could never be absolutely certain if their massive financial loss at the end of the day had been down to their own miscalculations at the beginning of it.

So, having managed to successfully fleece every single charity shop the length and breadth of the City of Portsmouth, Morose was £20,000 better off; but it meant the trip to Marks & Spencer had become more of a need than a want, just in case one of his elderly victims *hadn't* been suffering from the advanced stages of senile dementia and could therefore pick him out from a police line-up.

As he sat there, enjoying an extra-large cappuccino and a generously-sized slice of carrot cake, he was already feeling like a new man; but he continued to reflect on his next move. He knew that he needed a new identity, and he already had someone in mind to see about that; but he was still unsure as to what his next business venture would be.

It was then that he became aware of the crowd that had begun to gather outside the hotel next door. Like most people, he had a general awareness of the machinations of British politics, and therefore knew all too well about the UKIP party and what they stood for. With all the Brexit nonsense going on, he wasn't at all surprised to see that the gathering masses were there to proclaim their general objection.

By the time he'd moved on to his third coffee and slice of cake, the early evening's street performance was becoming most entertaining, to the point where he joined in with the others sitting outside the coffee shop with the occasional 'Oooh!' and 'Aaah' as they watched punches land and placards fly. When it all came to an end he even stood up to join the other spectators as they offered their appreciation with an enthusiastic round of applause along with the occasional 'BRAVO! BRAVO!'

Apart from providing him with something to look at other than his yacht, the not-so peaceful demonstration had given him an idea as to what his next career move could be. He'd no idea about how he'd go about becoming involved, but he was sure that it was something he could not only do, but excel at!

CHAPTER THIRTEEN
CATS AND BAGS

THE PRODUCTION meeting the following day was as busy as ever, with Eliot sitting at the head of the table and Martin to his right; but this morning's meeting was a little different, because Eliot seemed to have a rather obvious black eye, and his arm must have been broken as it was set in plaster and hung over his chest in a sling.

With a heavily bandaged head, and wearing a thick padded neck brace, Martin also looked a little worse for wear. Having both arrived by taxi, straight from Portsmouth Hospital's A&E department, they were still wearing the same clothes they had on the evening before, blood stains and all, and it seemed neither had had the chance to shave, either due to the constraints of time or pure physical inability.

Despite their injuries, they'd still managed to arrive before Abigail, who'd struggled to get out of bed that morning, and who eventually walked into the boardroom saying, 'Sorry I'm late.' It was only when she glanced up and saw Eliot and Martin at the far end of the long table that she said, 'Jesus Christ! What happened to you two?'

'They were beaten up by UKIP protestors,' said Marcus Thornbury, their Lead Anchor, an attractive older man in his late fifties who had a natural talent for reading from a teleprompter for hours on end, but little else.

'Yes, thank you, Marcus, but they were actually UKIP party members who mistook us for protestors. But anyway, shall we push on?' Eliot glared at Abigail, who was still standing beside the door, scanning the packed room looking for Will, and hoping he'd been kind enough to save a seat for her.

The evening before, having come to the conclusion that they'd sufficiently covered the UKIP demonstration, and deciding that Eliot and Martin must have left when the fighting had broken out, as they were nowhere to be seen, Will had been kind enough to take her out to a nearby Pizza Express. There they'd continued to get to know each other to the point where their date had ended as Abigail had hoped, with a snog outside her flat. Being the perfect gentlemen, Will had declined her offer of a coffee, and instead had asked if she'd like to go to the cinema with him on Friday night. Apparently they were showing the premier of the long-awaited sequel to the smash hit romantic comedy, *Twenty Seven Dresses*, called *Three Hundred and Sixty Five Handbags*.

Spotting him, and seeing that he had indeed saved her a seat, she squeezed over as everyone stared at her in an awkward silence.

'Are we *all* ready?' asked Eliot pointedly, clearly not in the best of moods.

'Yes, thank you,' she answered, sitting down beside Will and giving him a self-conscious little smile.

'Right then! First up, I'd like to introduce you all to Will. Will, er…'

For one heart-stopping moment, Will thought he was going to let the proverbial cat out of the bag by announcing to everyone what his surname was.

Fortunately for him, Eliot was just as embarrassed by Will's surname as Will was, and decided to simply say, '…our new cameraman, whose joined us from our friends over at the Portsmouth Post, and will be working alongside Abigail.'

The production team turned to stare at the young man sitting next to Abigail, who sent them a brave smile, desperately hoping that they'd all stop gawping at him.

'So!' continued Eliot, taking his own eyes off Will to glare at all those in attendance. 'What have you got for us today?'

A muted silence followed, which was generally the case, as everyone gazed around at each other, all hoping that someone else would be first to go.

It was Abigail who took the initiative by raising her hand.

'Yes!' said Eliot, pointing at her.

'We did a good piece on the UKIP, er, demonstration, yesterday evening which we emailed over to Martin.'

Hearing his name, Martin gently swivelled himself around so that he could face Abigail without having to twist his neck. 'Thank you, Abigail. I did receive it, and it's an excellent story. So I'd like to suggest that we run with it today.'

'I also thought,' she went on, 'that it may be worth doing a follow-up piece, about the growing rise of professional protestors being used for such demonstrations.'

'What did you have in mind?' asked Eliot.

'I thought I could have a go at interviewing the founder of the website, *WeProtestAnyDemonstration.com*. And then I could maybe follow a couple of their employees around, as they attended their various assignments.'

Putting his own rather embarrassing situation to one side, that of being the one who'd instigated the clash between UKIP supporters and UKIP demonstrators as he'd been stupid enough to say the word "bomb" out loud, and within such a politically charged public environment, Eliot said, 'Sounds good!'

However, Will wasn't quite so convinced, and believed that it could probably do with a little more thought, especially the bit about following a group of psychotic football supporters around to different political events for which they received a financial incentive if they could start a fight. He considered that he and Abigail had been lucky to have come out of yesterday's one unscathed, and had absolutely no intention of going to any more.

'Anything else from anyone?' asked Eliot, looking around the table at all his other employees.

Jenny Daily, fashion correspondent, raised her hand. 'The Prime Minister's niece, Claire Bridlestock, has just opened her own military fashion boutique in Winchester, and I'm going to interview her this afternoon.'

'OK, good. Anyone else?'

Jim Oakburn, social affairs correspondent, said, 'The Portsmouth Parents Association have put in another application to have HMS Victory turned into an adventure playground.'

'Didn't they apply for that last year?' asked Martin.

'I believe so. And the year before that as well.'

'You'd better cover it,' said Eliot, 'unless you've got anything else?'

'That's all I have, I'm afraid.'

'OK, who's next?'

Malcolm McDonald, sports correspondent, raised his hand.

'There's a girl who wants to do a sponsored swim to the Isle of Wight, but the council's saying she can't, as they think she'll probably be run over by at least one ferry. Anyway, the parents are a bit upset at being told what their daughter can, or cannot do, so they're taking the Council to court over it.'

'And that's sports news, is it?' asked Eliot.

'Well, the swimming bit is.'

'You'd better cover it, I suppose.'

Phil Packman, political correspondent, lifted his hand and, as delicately as he thought he could, asked, 'Do you want me to cover the UKIP Party Conference?'

Eliot and Martin exchanged glances, before Martin asked him, 'Surely they're going to cancel it, aren't they?'

'I doubt it. There may be quite a few still in A&E, but I can't imagine Michael Suntage not showing up, even if he has to be carried in on a stretcher!'

'Well, I suppose so,' said Eliot, who would have been happy if he never heard the word UKIP again. 'Right, is that it?'

'I'm afraid another dog went missing last night,' mentioned crime correspondent Declan Hacker.

'Oh no! Really?' said Martin, clearly upset to hear the news. 'Do you know what type it was?'

Checking his notes, Declan answered, 'They just said that it was a medium-sized one.'

'How about a name?'

Glancing down at his notes again, he came back with, 'Hatstand.'

'Poor thing,' lamented Martin.

Declan wasn't sure if he felt sorry for it because it had gone missing, or because it had a really stupid name; but either way, he was sick of having to report on every bloody missing dog story. The only reason there had been so many over the last few weeks was because of the recent trend of giving dogs the most ridiculous names imaginable, most of which were so embarrassing that a large percentage of owners had simply refused to go around calling after them when they'd run off to chase squirrels, or to stand around for hours on end smelling other dogs' bums. So the owners had just returned home to notify the police of their disappearance. 'Do I have to cover it?'

'I really think you should, yes!' said Martin, who was genuinely heartbroken each and every time he heard of another one going missing.

'You'd probably better,' agreed Eliot, 'but do please keep an eye out for something a little more salacious, preferably involving a murder, or a kidnapping. Even a robbery would do! And that goes for the rest of you,' he said, looking around the room. 'With Morose now dead, it's unlikely we're going to be handed any more stories on a plate, which means that we'll all need to start working a lot harder.' And to drive the message home, he continued to glare at everyone in the room for another few moments, before drawing the meeting to a close. 'OK, people. Be careful out there, and remember: don't take no for an answer, but don't take yes for one either!'

CHAPTER FOURTEEN
A PILLAR OF SOCIETY

MOROSE AWOKE on board his yacht to the sound of the sea gently lapping against the hull's side and the occasional squawk from a passing seagull. Once he'd shaved, showered and dressed in his new M&S suit, he took his motorised tender, along with a large wad of cash, back to shore for a pre-arranged meeting to discuss the details of his planned new identity.

The person he was due to see was Elizabeth Potts, a Fine Arts graduate who for a number of years had been a happily married Member of Parliament representing the London Borough of Lambeth. However, life hadn't gone exactly as planned, as she'd been one of the many politicians caught up in the 2009 parliamentary expenses scandal that saw her forced to swap her position as "pillar of society" to that of "girl propping up wall in prison". It had also cost her her marriage.

It was her two years stuck behind bars that had enabled her to study what was to become her new profession, forgery, and to specialise in providing criminals with new identities. She'd proved to be so good at it that by the time of her release she'd already grown a long list of appreciative clients, most of whom had been only too happy to recommend her services.

She'd been pleasantly surprised to find just how easy it was to set up in business, discovering it had distinct parallels with the oldest profession, that of prostitution. Both seemed to rely on word-of-mouth advertising, both only accepted cash, and as with a classy hooker who was prepared to bend over backwards to accommodate almost any need, she found herself to be in constant demand.

Another benefit was that she could run her business from home, saving her the cost of renting an office as well as the expense of commuting. Having found a humble three bed semi-detached house in Portsmouth that she could afford to buy for cash, she'd moved down to the south coast of England and put the word out that she was officially open for business.

It was because of her new residential location that Morose had come to hear of her, when he'd still been the Solent Police's Chief Inspector. Back then, despite knowing about Elizabeth Potts and what her line of work was, Morose had deliberately not taken any formal steps to have her arrested. After all, forgers never appeared on his list of people he needed to lock up in order to achieve his quarterly bonus, and generally speaking, professionals involved in helping others to gain new identities were left alone by both the police and the media. This was simply because they were far too useful, and nobody working within either sector of society ever really knew when they'd be in dire need of one.

Ringing Elizabeth Potts' front door bell, he didn't have to wait long before it was answered.

'Oh, hello, you must be Morose!' said a well-proportioned intelligent-looking lady with permed greying hair and a light blue twinset accessorised by a pearl necklace. With the bridge of her nose supporting a delicate pair of wire-framed glasses, she looked almost exactly like the head mistress of an all-girl's boarding school.

'And you must be Mrs Potts,' said Morose.

'Please, call me Elizabeth.'

'Good of you to see me at such short notice.'

'My pleasure. Do come in, won't you?' she invited, as she stepped aside to make way for him.

Morose glanced over both shoulders, as he'd found himself doing rather a lot recently; and satisfied that he hadn't been followed, he squeezed himself past his host.

Before closing the door, Elizabeth also peered outside, checking up and down the street for anything that looked out of place, like a white van with blacked-out windows and a satellite dish, or a man in a three-piece suit sitting on a low garden wall reading a copy of the Financial Times.

Confident that her road looked very much as it always did – a place where nothing much happened, she closed the door. 'Tea or coffee?'

'Coffee, please,' answered Morose, who'd already reached the end of the corridor.

'How'd you like it?' she asked, following after him.

'Milk, two sugars, please.'

'I'll fetch that for you now,' she said, as she watched him turn the corner to head into the dining room that she used as her office. She had to forcibly remind herself that her new client was no longer the Chief Inspector of the Solent Police, but was now better known as the Psychotic Serial Slasher of

Southampton and the South Coast, whose headless body had been washed up on Portsmouth Esplanade only the day before; and bearing that in mind, she felt that it was probably all right to leave him to have a wander around, and headed for the kitchen.

She retrieved a mug from the cupboard above the kettle, filled it three quarters full from the cafetière she'd already made for herself, added the milk and sugar, and after giving it a quick thirty-second blast in the microwave went to find her new client.

'Here you are!' she said to Morose, who seemed to be browsing through her classical CD collection.

Turning around, Morose used both hands to take the mug of steaming coffee. 'Thank you. So, how's business?' he asked, by way of making conversation.

'Oh, you know, up and down,' she answered. 'And how's life treating you now that you're dead?'

'So far, so good,' said Morose, taking a sip from his mug. 'But that's why I'm here, of course.'

'Yes, of course,' repeated Elizabeth, offering Morose a seat. 'So, am I safe to assume that you're looking for a new identity?'

'That's right,' he replied, as he made himself comfortable on the dining room chair that had been offered.

'OK, great! Now, we have three options available,' she said, reaching over the table to pick up a leaflet which she passed over to him. 'As you can see, we have our *Born Again* basic introductory package, for which we simply provide you with a new birth certificate. Then there's our *Ascension to Heaven* package, within which we include a passport, driver's license and a National Insurance number. And finally we have our *Sitting at God's Right Hand* package, which provides everything you could possibly need to start a whole new life, including a driver's licence, utility bills for proof of address, both personal and business bank accounts, a 32GB iPhone registered in your new name, a year's subscription to the *Radio Times*, the full range of social media profiles, and a paid TV licence along with your choice of *Virgin Media*, *Sky Digital* or *BT TV*.'

As Morose listened to the options, he glanced through the leaflet, paying particular attention to all the prices quoted. When she'd finished her initial sales pitch, he asked, 'Can I choose my own name?'

'You can choose from a selection of names, yes, but unfortunately you can't choose one at random.'

'That's a shame,' said Morose. 'May I ask why?'

'It's because we'll be providing you with the identity of someone who has already existed, but doesn't anymore, and who, had they still been living, would be the same age as you are now.'

'Oh, I see. So what choice do I have then?'

'Good question. Let me see,' and turning to her computer monitor, asked, 'What year were you born?'

'1959.'

'And are you planning on having a sex change?'

'I don't think so!' said Morose, clearly shocked by the very suggestion.

'Are you sure?' she asked, staring at Morose as if it was the expected norm for all her clients to have one.

'I'd most definitely prefer to stay as I am, if it's at all possible, yes!' answered Morose, who'd no intention of allowing himself to be persuaded otherwise.

'Right then,' said Elizabeth, returning to her monitor. 'So, to recap, you were born in 1959 and you'd like to keep your current sex. OK, here we are. It looks like you have four choices.'

'Only four?' asked Morose, who'd been expecting a couple of hundred, or at least ten.

'It's about average,' Elizabeth said. 'Shall I go through them?'

'If you could.'

Swivelling the monitor around so that Morose could see it as well, Elizabeth started to read through the list.

'Right. First we have Mr Dwayne Pipe, middle name Matthew. Then there's Mr Stan Still, middle name Mark. Third is Mr Seymour Legg, middle name Luke, and finally there's Mr Douglas McDongle, middle name John.' Elizabeth gazed expectantly at her client.

'Er,' said Morose. 'I don't mean to be funny, or anything, but aren't they all joke names?'

'I beg your pardon?'

'I mean, haven't they all just been made-up? Dwayne Pipe, Stan Still, Seymour Legg? They're all just comedy names, aren't they?'

'I can assure you, Mr Morose,' said Elizabeth, looking very much like someone who'd just been accused of cheating at bridge, 'that they are most definitely *not* "comedy names"!'

'Oh, sorry,' muttered Morose. 'I just thought that—' Seeing that he'd managed to offend the very woman he so desperately needed, he back-pedalled as best he could by saying, 'it's probably because they all sound so, um, realistic.'

'As I've explained, they *ARE* real names!' she said, almost raising her voice, and pulled the monitor back towards herself so that Morose couldn't see it anymore.

'Yes, sorry, of course.'

'So, do you want one or not?' she asked, still clearly put out.

'And there are really no more choices?'

'Well, if you had a sex change operation then yes, there would be a number of alternatives, but as you've made it emphatically clear that you're not prepared to do that, then sorry, no, that's all we have.'

Still adamant that he didn't want to become a woman, Morose tentatively asked, 'What was the last one again?'

'Mr Douglas John McDongle,' she answered, glancing back at the monitor.

'I'll think I'll take that one,' said Morose.

Using the mouse on the table in front of her, Elizabeth checked the box beside the relevant name. 'Are you sure?' she asked, looking over at him again. 'Once I hit the enter button, there's no going back.'

'What was it again?' questioned Morose. Now that the time had come, he really wasn't too keen on being called anything other than Morose, a name he'd grown a liking to over the years.

With a heavy sigh, Elizabeth repeated, 'Mr Douglas John McDongle.'

'And that's definitely the only one you have?'

'Apart from the other three, yes!'

'All right,' said Morose, already experiencing some regret for having faked his own death in quite such a convincing manner. 'I'll take it!'

Elizabeth hit the ENTER key.

'Right then,' she said, looking a little happier. 'Have you decided which package you'd like?'

'Oh, er, yes,' said Morose. 'I think I'll have the third option.'

'Our *Sitting at the Right Hand of God* one?' she asked, for confirmation.

'Yes, that one.'

'OK,' and using the mouse again, she checked the box besides the third option before pressing ENTER once more. 'Right. That'll be £14,500 please.'

'Do you need it all now?'

'Well, if you're a little short, I suppose I can take half now and half when you pick it up.'

'And how long until it's ready?'

She glanced down at her watch. 'As long as I can take some of the money now, you'll be able to pick it up tomorrow morning.'

'That soon?'

'Well, yes. Most of our clients do generally seem to be in a bit of a hurry.'

Morose wasn't surprised, and from the back pocket of his suit trousers he pulled a huge wedge of £50 notes. 'I only brought £10,000,' he said, as he laid it down on the table, 'but the rest is accessible, and I'll bring it with me tomorrow.'

'That's fine,' said Elizabeth. 'Let me get you a receipt.'

Pulling a pre-printed pad with carbon duplicates

towards her, along with a Bic biro, she asked, 'What's the date today?'

'It's the 23rd.'

As Elizabeth finished filling out the receipt, out of curiosity she asked, 'So, what are your plans once you've become Mr Douglas John McDongle?'

Morose shuddered at hearing the name, but knowing that he'd just have to get used to it, said, 'I'm not exactly sure, but I hear MPs do all right, so I was thinking about maybe making a move into politics.'

'Oh, right!' said Elizabeth, with clear interest. 'Did you know that I used to be the MP for Lambeth?'

'I'd heard it mentioned, yes.'

'And which party would you be looking to represent?'

'Probably the Conservatives,' replied Morose. 'They seem to be quite popular at the moment.'

'The world does seem to be leaning a little to the right these days, especially with what's going on in America.'

'But what I don't know,' continued Morose, 'is how to go about becoming one.'

'What, a Conservative? I think it's fairly straight forward. You just have to favour the rich over the poor, support fox hunting and say that you're against immigration, as long as it doesn't have an adverse effect on our free trade agreements with the EU.'

'No, I meant, how I'd go about becoming an MP?'

'Oh, that! Well, yes, it can seem a little complicated. Let me see if I can remember. First you have to register your candidature - you'll need a nomination form from the local council to do that. And then you simply fill it out and hand it back in with a £500 deposit, along with the signatures of ten electors.'

'Ten electors?'

'Yes, that's right. From the party you're intending to represent, but I could probably sort that out for you.'

'You could?'

'I don't see why not. Oh, and you'd also need to wait for a general election, which probably won't be for another couple of years. The alternative, of course, is that there's a by-election, but for that to happen a current local MP would have to resign, or go to prison, or something like that, at which point you'd need an election agent.'

'An election agent?'

'I'm afraid so. It's just one of the rules. Every candidate has to have one. They run the campaign for you and manage your accounts. Now there is the option for you to act as your own agent, but I wouldn't recommend it, not if you've never stood before.'

'I see,' said Morose. 'I must admit that it does sound more complicated than I'd been expecting.'

Elizabeth leaned back in her chair and gazed over at her client with a look of sagacious contemplation. 'If you're serious about this, then I could probably act as an agent for you.'

'You could?'

'Well, yes, I suppose. But it would have to be on a ten percent commission basis though, calculated against your earnings when you became an MP.'

'Oh, right. And how much do you think I'd make?'

'I believe the current salary is £74,000.'

'Is that all?'

'Not much, I know. But it's not the main source of a politician's income of course. A good one makes more by "representing their electorate".'

'And how would you "represent your electorate"?' asked Morose, who wasn't even sure what an electorate was, let alone how to represent one.

'Oh, you know, helping certain investors within the community to gain special planning permission, or to favour one particular tender over another. That sort of thing.'

'You mean by accepting bribes,' said Morose, who was more than familiar with the practice from his days as a police chief inspector.

'It's not the official term, of course, but it amounts to the same thing, yes. Now if, perchance, you were to ever land the top job,' Elizabeth continued, 'then the world really would be your oyster, financially speaking.'

'And why's that?' asked Morose.

'Well, take a look at the current Prime Minister, our very own Robert Bridlestock. He only draws a salary of £140,000 a year, but since being elected he's become the richest man in the UK, and now has an estimated net worth of over £14 billion!'

It was at that point Morose realised that he'd clearly been in the wrong line of work all these years. As he tried to get his head around just how much £14 billion was, and if it would fit on board his yacht, he cleared his throat and said, 'You know what, I think I'd definitely like to become an MP, and for you to become my electoral agent.'

Elizabeth smiled at him. 'From what I've heard

about you, I think you'd make an excellent politician. Tell you what, as soon as I've sorted out your new identity, I suggest we start thinking of ways we could force a by-election, and then how best to go about raising awareness of your candidature.'

'So, you'd be happy to be my agent, then?'

'For ten percent of what I suspect you could earn, it's a deal,' and they both stood up to shake hands on their new business partnership.

CHAPTER FIFTEEN
MARGERY AND ETHEL

A BIGAIL HAD ONLY just had a chance to sit down at her desk, take a sip from the coffee that Will had been kind enough to make for her, log onto Facebook, reply to all the friends who'd messaged her since she'd woken up, scrolled through her Facebook Timeline, liked and commented on the various items that had been posted, popped over to Twitter, did very much the same thing there, checked the Tinder app on her mobile, had a casual scroll down the men currently on offer, open up her personal email account on her desktop, reply to an urgent message from her mum about the new living room curtains she was ordering, check her business email account and delete all the junk mail that hadn't been automatically filtered into her spam file, ask Will if he'd be kind enough to make her another coffee, and start to type the name, *WeProtestAnyDemonstration*.com into her browser, when her desk phone rang.

Picking up the receiver, she said, 'Abigail Love speaking?' and took the opportunity to stare at Will as he placed a fresh cup of coffee on her desk.

'Hello, Abigail, it's Eliot here. How's that story about those professional demonstrators coming along?'

'Really well, thank you,' she said, as she finished typing and hit the ENTER key.

'That's good, but I don't suppose you and Will

could take a break from that to cover a store theft in town?'

'Yes, of course.'

'It took place sometime yesterday, at a charity shop in Cascades.'

'Which one?' asked Abigail, as she knew that there were quite a few in that area.

'It's the Blind Dogs for the Guides one, near Safebusy's.'

'I think I know it,' she said. She didn't, but didn't think it would be too hard to find, and anyway, she always preferred to be out and about than stuck behind a desk doing boring research. 'We'll head down there straight away.'

Ending the call, she said to Will, who'd only just sat down, 'Grab your coat, we've got a story to cover.'

'Whereabouts?' asked Will, who up until then had had a busy morning updating his LinkedIn profile with his new job details.

'A charity shop's been robbed, down in Cascades Shopping Centre.'

'Which one?' he asked as he stood up to put his suit jacket on.

'Blind Dogs for the Guides.'

'I think I know it,' he said. He'd also never heard of it before, but wasn't keen to admit it.

They both reached over to turn their computer monitors off, and headed for the door.

About forty-five minutes later, having parked in Safebusy's customer car park that was free on the premise that you bought something from them at some stage during your stay, they found the charity shop in question and pushed open the door, setting off a tiny bell at the top in the process.

Stepping inside, they were greeted by that musty, all-too familiar smell that seemed to permeate through every charity shop the length and breadth of the British Isles.

Seeing two old ladies perched behind the counter, one with permed silver hair and the other with the same style but with a blue rinse, Abigail made her way over with Will following behind.

'May I help you, my dear?' asked the nearest lady, the one with the silver hair.

Holding up her press pass, Abigail said, 'If you could. My name's Abigail Love, from Hampshire Today. I understand that there's been a robbery?'

'Has there?' asked the lady.

'That's what we've been told, yes.'

'I'd better ask my colleague. She'll probably know something about it. Hold on,' and she swivelled around in her chair to speak to the lady with the blue rinse sitting next to her.

'Oh, hello, Ethel. I didn't see you there. Did you know that there's been a robbery?'

'Really?'

'That's what this nice young lady said.'

'Was it somewhere nearby?'

'I'm not sure. Let me ask her,' and she swivelled back again. 'Where did you say it happened?'

'It took place here, at this shop.'

'Here?'

'Yes, that's right.'

'At this shop?'

'Right again.'

'Gosh! I'd better tell my colleague. Wait there for just a moment, and I'll see if I can find her,' and she turned, and with a start, said, 'Ethel! There you are. I was just looking for you. Did you know that we'd been robbed?'

'What, today?'

'I don't think so, but there's a nice young lady at the front of the shop who may know. Now don't go anywhere, and I'll see if I can find her.' Once more she swivelled round in her chair.

'Oh, you're here! Do you know if it happened today?'

Abigail sighed.

'No, it was sometime yesterday.'

'Yesterday, did you say?'

'That's right, yesterday.'

'I'm not sure if I was even here yesterday. Hold on, let me ask my colleague.'

'*Jesus fucking Christ,*' said Abigail, under her breath.

Having found her blue-haired colleague once more, the lady said, 'Hello, Ethel. Do you know if I was here yesterday?'

'Yes, Margery. You were here, with me.'

'Oh yes, of course, that's right, silly me,' and with an amused smile, Margery turned back to Abigail. 'Apparently, I was here yesterday after all!'

'So, you remember calling the police then?'

'The police?'

'That's right! Do you remember calling them, when you were robbed?'

'When who was robbed?'

'When *you* were robbed?'

'When *I* was robbed?' she asked, with a look of alarm.

'Not you, personally. When the shop was robbed.'

'Which one?'

'This one!'

'This one, what?'

'*This shop!*'

'I'm sorry my dear, but you've completely lost me.'

Abigail gave Will a look of earnest desperation.

'Shall I have a go?' he asked.

Moving to one side she said, 'Be my guest.'

Stepping forward, Will smiled at the first old lady, Margery, the one with silver permed hair, and said, 'Hello!' with a smile.

'Oh, hello! You're a nice looking young man. Are you two together?'

'Oh, er, well,' and he glanced over at Abigail. 'We're both from Hampshire Today, if that's what you mean.'

'That's nice. And what's that then?'

'Sorry, what's what?'

'Hampshire Today? Is it one of those new religious organisations?'

'Er, no. It's a YouTube news channel.'

'Oh yes, of course. A bit like those Jehovah's Witnesses, I suppose. You know, you remind me a bit of my husband. He was a Christian Scientist, you know, but he passed away some years ago now, God rest his soul. Your name's not Alfred, by any chance?'

'Er, no. It's Will.'

'Oh dear. That's a shame. Never mind. He believed

in re-incarnation you see, or at least I think he did, so I just thought that he may have come back as you, and I haven't even had a chance to do my hair yet,' she said, giving it a quick prod, just to make sure it was still there.

'OK, well, I'm afraid I'm not him. Sorry about that.'

'Never you mind, my dear. It's certainly not your fault. But I must say that you do look familiar. What's your surname?'

'Look, we really just wanted to talk to you about—'

'Are you two married?' asked the lady, somewhat out of the blue.

Will and Abigail exchanged a brief look of amused embarrassment.

Turning back to her, and keen to move the subject on from either what his surname was, or the current status of his relationship with Abigail, Will said, 'As I mentioned before, we only work together, nothing more.'

'You prefer men then?' asked the lady. 'I knew a gay once. He used to work as a stable boy. Bernie, I think his name was. Or was it Gerald? I can't remember, but you look a little like him as well. Anyway, he was arrested for it, but I understand it's legal these days?'

'Well, as I'm not one, I'm not sure I'd know.'

'You're not sure if you know?' she asked. 'Then I suggest you marry the girl. As I said, you look good together, and I'm sure she wouldn't mind if you were a bit gay, would you, my dear?' she asked, looking directly at Abigail, who just stared straight back, unsure as to how to respond.

Turning to Abigail, Will asked, 'Is there anything

else you'd like me to ask this nice old lady?'

Abigail couldn't even remember why they'd come in the first place. 'Not that I can think of,' she said, and now found herself looking at Will, with renewed concerns about his sexual orientation.

'Right then,' said Will, who'd had quite enough of both the conversation and having to spend quite so long inside a charity shop, and so turned to the old lady with the silver hair and said, 'Thank you very much for your time. You've been most helpful.'

'Not at all, my dear,' said Margery, as Will and Abigail headed back out of the door.

Once outside, Abigail said, 'Well, that was a complete waste of time!'

'They weren't very helpful, were they?'

'I've had more intelligent conversations with a couple of goldfish. But still,' she continued, 'we need to make a report or else Eliot will want to know what the hell we've been up to.'

They went through what was becoming a routine, and when both were ready, Abigail faced Will's iPhone.

'This is Abigail Love, reporting from outside a fashion boutique shop in the heart of Portsmouth from where, only yesterday afternoon, a gang of dangerous criminals armed with an assortment of machineguns, shotguns and other types of guns, forced their way inside. After threatening the lives of various members of staff, they made off with a large amount of cash and the shop's entire collection of shoes, dresses and handbags, whose brands included Prada, Dolce & Gabbana, Gucci, Armani, Louis

Vuitton, and Manolo Blahnik, to name but a few. Since then Police have issued a statement telling people that if anyone sees three men in their late twenties wandering around town dressed in either brown removal men's overalls, or something infinitely more fashionable, under no circumstances should they try to make a citizen's arrest, but instead to call them on the usual number. This is Abigail Love reporting. Back to the studio.'

After fixing a look of serious intent at Will's iPhone for the standard five second count, she took a deep breath, looked up at Will and said, 'Not my best, but it will do.'

CHAPTER SIXTEEN
A NEW BORN KING

L ATER THAT afternoon there was a knock at Eliot's door, followed by the appearance of Jean, the office manager.

'There's a Mr Douglas McDongle here to see you,' she announced.

Eliot looked up from his desk. 'Who?'

'A Mr Douglas McDongle. He said he's here to talk to you about doing some promotional advertising.'

'Well, you'd better show him in then!' said Eliot, who'd just been going over his projected cash flow forecast for the following quarter, which wasn't looking good.

Standing well clear of the door, Jean turned to look upwards, and then with her eyes wide and mouth half open, gestured for their visitor to enter.

Eliot had never had anyone walk in off the street to ask about placing some advertising with them before, and waited with baited breath to see what sort of person it would be.

He wasn't disappointed.

The man who lumbered in was an immense bald-headed chap, and Eliot could see why Jean had given him quite such a wide berth, as his vast physical mass could barely fit through the door. Not only was his size impressive, but his appearance was equally so. He was wearing an immaculate dark blue suit, a pair of highly polished black leather shoes, a pristine white shirt and a polka dot blue tie that had been perfectly secured with a large Windsor knot. He looked as if he'd just come back from some exotic part of the world where the weather was always fine, as he had a quite remarkable sun tan. As the figure smiled at him, Eliot couldn't help but notice his brilliant white teeth that stood out against his giant-sized orange head, like a white picket fence that some crafty property investor had just had erected around an exclusive off-plan housing development on Mars.

The day before, Morose had taken the advice of his new electoral agent who, before saying goodbye to him at the door, had advised him that if he wasn't prepared to have a sex change operation, then he should at least make some sort of an effort to alter his appearance. So, after picking up his new identity pack that very morning, Morose had made a quick trip to the Bright'n White dentistry in town, followed by a visit to Tanya's All Natural Tanning Boutique next door. Gone for good was Morose, the Psychotic Slasher of Southampton and the South Coast, and instead emerged His Immenseness, Mr Douglas John McDongle, a man who could have easily been mistaken for a new born king.

Standing in awe of the figurehead looming up before him, Eliot reached over his desk, and taking hold of Mr Douglas McDongle's outstretched orangey-brown hand, eventually managed to say, 'Welcome to Hampshire Today. My name's Eliot Bespoke. I understand that you might like to do some promotional advertising with us?'

Still showing off his brand new smile, Morose, now

calling himself McDongle, said, 'Well, I wanted to chat to you about the possibility of undertaking a mutually beneficial collaborative business agreement.'

'You can go now, thank you,' Eliot said to Jean, who hadn't moved from her position besides the door, as she'd been unable to take her eyes off of their guest since his grand entrance, and now seemed to have become transfixed by the back of his giant, heavily sun-tanned bald head.

Snapping herself out of the trance she found herself in, she apologised, saying. 'Sorry, yes of course,' adding, 'I'll leave you to it,' and slunk out to secure the door behind her.

'Take a seat, won't you?' offered Eliot.

McDongle looked down to examine the chair on offer, which seemed to be sturdy enough, so he accepted the invitation and made himself comfortable.

'So, what is it that you had in mind?' asked Elliot, resuming his own seat.

'I'm intending to stand in Portsmouth and Gosport's forthcoming by-election, but as an unknown political figure, my election agent has recommended that I run what she described as "positive news stories".'

'Right,' said Eliot. 'Although I must admit that I didn't know that there was going to be a by-election.'

'It hasn't been officially announced yet,' said McDongle, 'but it will be happening at some point over the next few weeks.'

'Excellent!' exclaimed a more than delighted Eliot, as he picked up a pen whilst searching his desk for something to write on. 'And which party are you planning to represent?' he asked, as he turned over the back of the latest viewing figures report.

'Conservatives.'

'Isn't that Michael Brownfield's seat?' asked Eliot.

'So I'm told.'

'I see. Sorry. I didn't know he'd resigned.'

'He hasn't.'

'He's been taken ill then?'

'I don't think so.'

'Don't tell me he's been sacked?' asked Eliot, with hopeful expectation for a half-decent story.

'Not that I'm aware of.'

'So, if you don't mind me asking, how're you going to run in his place if he's still the MP for Portsmouth and Gosport?'

'I apologise,' said McDongle. 'I'm not making myself clear. He hasn't stood down yet, but I'm confident that he will, and any day now, and at that point a by-election will be announced.'

Eliot stared across at the man with the white teeth and the large orange head, who simply smiled straight back. Clearly the man knew something he didn't, and keen to find out what it was, asked, 'And how is it that you know that, may I ask?'

McDongle shrugged. 'I just do. But in part, that's what I wanted to talk to you about.'

'Oh, right, well. I'm all ears!' said Eliot, as he sat up in his chair like a rabbit on a night time adventure over to the central reservation of the M4.

Douglas rested his hands in his lap, sat forward a little and said, 'I was hoping that Hampshire Today would be able to…support my campaign, so to speak.'

'I see,' said Eliot, who knew exactly what he meant. 'And in exchange for running a series of favourable news items about you, what could we expect in return?'

McDongle paused for a moment, gave Eliot another beaming great smile and said, 'News!'

'News?'

'That's correct.'

'And, er, what sort of "news" would you be able to provide us with?'

'Oh, you know, the sort that would attract large numbers of viewers followed by a heavy influx of corporate advertisers.'

Eliot's heart picked up a beat. If the man before him was suggesting what he thought he was, then he was most definitely entering into uncharted, but highly profitable, waters. And so, to help clarify what was being proposed, he asked, 'Am I right in saying that if we provide your campaign with favourable coverage, you'll be able to provide us with stories?'

'Exclusive stories, yes!'

CHAPTER SEVENTEEN
THIRTY TWO POUNDS AND
HOW MUCH?

'DO YOU KNOW what this film's about?' asked Will, in a conversational tone, as Abigail and he waited patiently in the queue inside the vast lobby of Portsmouth's Odeon Cinema complex.

'It's the sequel to *Twenty Seven Dresses*,' replied Abigail, as if that was sufficient information to explain its plot, and the twelve other films that were likely to follow.

'Oh, right!' said Will. 'And what was that about?'

'You haven't seen *Twenty Seven Dresses*?' she asked, in surprise and disbelief. She'd never met anyone before who hadn't, not that she knew of. But if he'd not, which she didn't think was possible, but on the off-chance, it at least answered one question. There was just no way he was gay! She knew this for a fact because, according to extensive research conducted by Hot Magazine, there wasn't a single homosexual man living in the Western Hemisphere who hadn't seen it at least once. And this made good sense, as it had the highest wedding count of any film that had been made, ever, and by a long way.

'Not that I can remember,' answered Will, which was at least honest. He'd sat through numerous rom com-type films when there'd been nothing else to watch on TV, but unless they'd stood out in some way either through the clever use of ultra-extreme violence, or the visually stimulating display of close-up sex, it was unlikely that he'd be able to differentiate one from the other.

'Oh, you must have,' said Abigail, still not convinced. 'It's been on TV loads of times. It's that one where the girl had the crush on her boss, who started dating her sister, and they were going to get married, which made her even more upset, but then she realised that she loved this other guy, the one who'd written a really nasty story about her in a magazine. But as it turned out, he loved her too, but didn't realise he did until half way through, so it all worked out rather well for everyone in the end.'

As far as Will could tell, Abigail's summary sounded like every other wedding-type rom com that had ever been made since *Four Weddings and a Funeral*, but just to show that he was at least listening, asked, 'So, where did the twenty seven dresses come in to it then?'

'They were from the weddings she'd been to as a bridesmaid that she kept stuffed inside this built-in wardrobe, but she had so many that she could never close the doors, and they kept bursting out whenever she had someone round to visit.'

'Sounds like she needed a bigger wardrobe.'

'You really haven't seen it, have you?'

'I don't think so, no, sorry. But I'm sure I would have liked it, if I had.'

There was no response from Abigail to that, and as they shuffled forward with the queue in what now felt like an awkward silence, Will thought he'd better say something, so he asked, 'What was this one called again?'

'Three Hundred and Sixty Five Handbags!' she answered, unimpressed that he couldn't even remember the name of the film he'd asked her to see.

'Oh yes, that's right.'

But then he realised that he may have displayed a little insensitivity towards some films that sounded as if they could easily become her all-time favourites. And given the fact that he was really hoping to be able to have sex with her that night, with about as much sincerity as he could muster, he said, 'Well anyway, I can't wait to see this one. It does sound *really* good!'

But it hadn't come out right, more like he was just taking the piss, which was evident by Abigail's reaction, as she folded her arms and turned her head away to examine a film poster that she couldn't possibly have had any genuine interest in, as it was called *Zombies, Warmed Up.*

Sensing the mistake he'd made, Will thought he'd better come up with something by way of an apology, and fast, as they were nearly at the ticket counter.

'OK, look,' he said, 'to be honest, Abi, it's probably not my sort of film, but I wanted to take you to see something that I thought *you* would like, not necessary one that I wanted to see.'

That did make sense to Abigail, just about, and with the apology accepted, she unfolded her arms and put one of them through his to give it a bit of a squeeze. She was falling for him, she knew she was, and the fact that he didn't like the sound of a couple of films that featured a wardrobe crammed full of fluffy wedding-type dresses and a flat littered with Gucci handbags probably wasn't a bad thing.

'Well, OK,' she said, 'but next time I suggest we go and see something we'd both like,' and she gazed up into his dreamy dark brown eyes, and added, 'Agreed?'

'Agreed,' he said, feeling himself stir both emotionally and physically. He was falling for her as well, there was no question about that - and that was despite the fact that she was still the girl who'd made his life hell on earth at school.

They held on to each other as they edged ever nearer to the ticket counter; but as they did so he began to worry about what would happen when she did eventually find out that he was Richard Will Wankett. And for the briefest of moments he was right back at Whitworth School, hearing the very same girl who was now holding on to his arm ask him, *'Where's your blankett, Wee Willy Wankett?'*

He shuddered at the memory.

'Are you OK?' asked Abigail.

'Yes, fine. It's just a bit cold in here. I'll be alright once we're inside.' He looked down at the beautiful girl who was looking back at him with her luminescent blue eyes. *Maybe she wouldn't even remember me?* he thought. *Maybe there were two Abigail Loves who grew up in Gosport?* Both were possible, but neither very likely.

With his mind elsewhere they stepped up to the counter, and suddenly realising that it was his turn to ask for tickets, said, 'Two for *Three Hundred and*, er…'

He could feel Abigail's arm tighten around his, but didn't dare look at her.

The lady behind the till smiled at him with amused pity. After all, he was hardly the first man she'd served that evening who couldn't remember the exact number of handbags to be featured in the film; so she helped him by finishing off what he was clearly trying to say.

'*Three Hundred and Sixty Five Handbags?*'

'Yes! That's the one!' said Will, with relief.

'And would you like to sit together?' asked the lady, as she looked down at her screen.

No, we'd like to sit really far apart, was the most obvious answer he could think of, but refraining from using what he personally considered to be the highest form of wit, that of acute belittling sarcasm, instead answered, 'Together, yes, please,' and felt Abigail's arm soften.

'OK! There you are. Row G, seat numbers 94 and 95. That will be thirty-two pounds and fifty pence, please.'

Thirty-two pounds and how much? You must be fucking joking? asked Will, but fortunately not out loud.

It had been a while since he'd last been to the cinema.

Digging out his wallet from his jeans pocket, he said, 'Yes, of course,' and with a thin smile, pulled out his Instathon Credit Card. He shielded his embossed name from Abigail, and his pin number from everyone else, paid for the tickets, returned the card to his wallet and the wallet to his pocket. He took the two tickets being held out for him, gave the lady behind the counter a begrudging smile, and let Abigail escort him towards the relevant entrance, hoping to God that the evening was going to be worth it.

CHAPTER EIGHTEEN
A BIT OF A SHOCK

AFTER WHAT he'd considered to be a highly successful meeting with Hampshire Today, it was time for Mr Douglas John McDongle, who was still trying to get used to his new name, to instigate his plan to become a Conservative Member of Parliament.

It had taken him a while to work out exactly how he was going to do it, and had even asked for Elizabeth's advice, but now that he had, he was supremely confident that it would work.

It was going to be a three-pronged attack, to which he'd given the code name Operation Superglue, the first part of which was to wholly and unequivocally discredit the man who stood in his way, the current Conservative MP for Portsmouth and Gosport, Mr Michael Brownfield, to the point where he'd be forced to resign from his position, or be sacked.

The second part was directly linked to the first: to do all that he could to ensure that his main opponent in the subsequent enforced by-election would have absolutely no chance of winning against him.

And the third was to do parts one and two in such a way that he'd guarantee that Hampshire Today had all the stories they'd need for him to meet his side of their agreement, so that they'd give him the headline support necessary for him to win the seat.

So, with that in mind, all McDongle had to do was to focus on parts one and two, and the third part should take care of itself.

That evening, as Abigail and Will were finding their seats to begin watching *Three Hundred and Sixty Five Handbags*, McDongle was emerging from the local YouGet store having picked up most of the items on his list, which included some K-Y Jelly, a tube of superglue, a camcorder, a beginner's bondage set, and a 30,000 volt stun gun. He already had the other three on his list; the phone number of a local male escort agency, one which catered for both gay and straight sex, a Conservative Party Rosette, and Michael Brownfield's address.

A short taxi ride took him to 6, Hellene Road, just off Eastern Parade, where Mr Brownfield's Edwardian detached house was situated.

Jumping out of the cab, McDongle bounded up the steps to the front door, with all the enthusiasm of a dog chasing a postman. Making sure his rosette was in place and carefully removing the stun gun from his YouGet shopping bag, he pressed the button on the white plastic video intercom system that they must have had installed for security reasons.

After a few moments, a man's voice responded with a monosyllabic, *'Yes?'*

'Oh, hello!' said McDongle, beaming a wide grin at the little camera he could see. 'I've just popped around to see who you'll be voting for in the next general election,' and just in case there was any doubt regarding either his sincerity, or his credentials, showed the camera his giant-sized rosette.

That did the trick; the door opened immediately and McDongle was met by an average-looking middle-aged man with a crumpled grey face and equally crumpled grey hair. It was Mr Michael Brownfield himself.

'Well, hello there!' he said, just about as cheerfully as was physically possible. 'It's good to see one of our own out on the campaign trail, but you're a little early, aren't you? There won't be another election for at least two years!'

'I've only just become a party member,' answered McDongle, 'so I thought I'd get some practice in.'

'Well, good for you, but you're preaching to the converted, I'm afraid. I'm Michael Brownfield, the Conservative MP for Portsmouth and Gosport.'

'*You're* Michael Brownfield?' asked McDongle, with plausible surprise.

'Yes, that's right! I am he! The very same!'

'Well I never! So I suppose it's a bit pointless of me asking who you're going to vote for?'

As soon as they'd stopped chuckling about the circumstances of the situation, McDongle asked, somewhat out of the blue, 'Is your wife in?'

Catching Michael completely by surprise, he answered, 'Who, Sandra? Er, yes. Why? Do you know her?'

'Not yet,' replied McDongle. 'And how about your children?'

'We don't have any! Look, what's this all about?' asked Michael, taking a half-step backwards.

'I must apologise. I haven't formally introduced myself. My name's Douglas McDongle, and I'm going to be standing as the Conservative Party candidate in the forthcoming by-election.'

'I beg your pardon?' asked Michael, thinking that he must have misheard that, or at least misunderstood.

'As I said, my name's Douglas McDongle, and I'm going to be standing as the Conservative Party candidate in the forthcoming by-election.'

'I think you'll find that there isn't a by-election coming up, as I've got no intention of standing down!'

'Yes, I'm sure, but I'm here to change your mind.' After a furtive glance over his shoulder, McDongle held down his stun gun's arming button and gave Mr Brownfield a generous three second blast. This was clearly a bit of a shock to the MP, mainly because he hadn't expected it, but also because of the 30,000 volts which were enough to incapacitate him to the point where he simply keeled over backwards.

With another glance over his shoulder, McDongle entered the house, stepped over the body, and dragged it backwards far enough so that its feet were clear of the door which he closed before going in search of the man's wife.

'MRS BROWNFIELD?' he called. 'MRS BROWNFIELD?'

A woman's voice echoed from somewhere towards the back of the house.

'I'M IN THE KITCHEN.'

McDongle followed the voice until he emerged into their visually stunning open plan kitchen, where she appeared to be engrossed in the creation of something that needed a lot of flour.

Glancing up and seeing the rosette, she naturally assumed that the giant bald-headed heavily-suntanned man with the grinning white teeth was one of her husband's colleagues, and said, 'Forgive me, but I'm practicing for Portsmouth's Celebrity Bake Off.' Returning her attention to the setting of a timer, she added, 'I'm not very good, I'm afraid. I can hardly make a sandwich, let alone a Bakewell Tart.' Then she thought of something funny, and said, 'More like a Baked-Badly Tart!' and shrieked with laughter at her own joke.

'I'm a bit of a cook myself,' lied McDongle, with enthusiasm.

'Oh, are you? Well, perhaps you can come around here and tell me what I'm doing wrong then.'

With gracious acceptance of her invitation, he lumbered his way around to the other side of the central area, re-charging the stun-gun as he went.

CHAPTER Nineteen
A CRITICAL Review

ABIGAIL AND WILL emerged from the dimly lit cinema like a couple of loved-up hedgehogs waking up from their annual hibernation, keen to get on with life's many necessities, well, one of them at least.

'I'll walk you home,' offered Will, as he thought a perfect gentleman would, but secretly hoping that she'd then invite him up to her flat for some "coffee", as she had the last time.

He'd politely declined then, but only because he hadn't expected to be asked and, subsequently, wasn't as prepared as he should have been. But since then he'd picked up a family-sized packet of sensitive, pro-relief, micro-stimulating, Fair Trade, organic and fully bio-degradable condoms that were on special offer at Safebusy's, and was keen to give at least one of them a go.

As they strolled towards her flat, arm in arm, he asked her, 'So, did you enjoy the film?'

'Very much so, thank you! How about you?'

'It was all right.'

He'd intended that to have come out with a little more enthusiasm than it actually had, and so to help convince her that he really *had* enjoyed it, tagged, 'I suppose,' on to the end.

But he'd made a poor case for convincing Abigail as

117

to his rapturous adoration of the film, as he probably should have done, and not surprisingly she came back at him with, 'And which part of it *didn't* you enjoy, exactly?' with a discernible edge to her voice.

Refraining from answering, 'All of it,' as he'd have liked, and certainly not too keen to admit that he'd dozed off shortly after the title sequence had finished, and had only woken up when the house lights had come back on, he said, 'Oh, I liked *every* part! It was all *really* good, and much better than I was expecting!'

Fortunately for Will, Abigail had been so engrossed in the film that she'd been oblivious to the fact that her date for the night had used the occasion to catch up on some sleep.

'It's a shame you hadn't seen *Twenty Seven Dresses* first,' she said. 'It would have helped you to understand the history between Jane and her sister, and why she felt she had to start buying all those handbags.'

But unless the plotline of a Hollywood film was able to permeate the consciousness of someone experiencing a two hour pattern of deep sleep, known scientifically as SWS, which is the third stage of non-rapid eye movement, it was unlikely that Will would have even known that the film featured actual people. As far as he was concerned, judging by the title, it was more likely to have been about some genetically mutated handbags that had been engineered at a molecular level to breed like rabbits.

'What was your favourite part?' asked Abigail, clearly intent on having a more in-depth conversation about it than Will was either willing, or able, to.

He thought fast. 'I must admit, Abi, you're right. I did struggle to understand it all. I really should have made the effort to see *Twenty Seven Dresses* first. I don't suppose you could explain what happened?'

'Of course I can,' she said, smiling up at him. 'Well, after they got married, in the first film, Kevin's editor asked him to do an article about her sister, Tess, the pretty blonde one who had the hair in a high bun with a braided wraparound. Tess had already agreed to buy one handbag every day for a year as a social experiment, to see if doing so would change her in any way. But then Jane became jealous of the amount of time Kevin was spending with Tess for the story, as well as her growing collection of handbags, so she also started to buy one a day, hoping that Kevin would do the story about her instead of her sister. But when Kevin's editor found out that he's now got two sisters, each trying to buy a better handbag than the other on a daily basis, he asked him to do the article about sibling rivalry as demonstrated by the handbag-buying competition going on between them. But then, about half way through the…'

'Isn't this your place?' interrupted Will, who'd become desperate for Abigail to stop talking about the many complexities of a film he now thought should have come with a Government Mental Health Warning advising all heterosexual men not to watch it under any circumstances, even if it *could* result in them getting laid.

Clearing her throat, Abigail asked, 'Would you like to come up for some coffee?' about as casually as it was possible for her to.

Will was on the verge of having sex, with a real-life woman as well, and one who just also happened to be exceptionally attractive. With that much longed-for expectation, there was absolutely no way he was going to say what he'd have liked, which was, *As long as you're not going to continue to go on about a film that sounds only slightly more interesting than a documentary about flower arranging.* Instead he simply smiled at her and said, 'That would be nice, thank you!'

And with that, Abigail took hold of his hand and led him up the steps to the communal front door, where she stopped to begin exploring the deepest darkest recesses of her handbag in search of her keys.

CHAPTER TWENTY
CALLING FOR A TAXI

ABIGAIL LAID HER head on Will's chest, listening to the rhythm of his heart return to more normal levels. They'd just had the most wonderful sex, and although he hadn't hit all the right spots at the right time, or even in the right order, and despite the fact that he'd had two goes at it, coming three times in the process, once by accident at the very beginning, and that she herself hadn't been granted a single orgasm, it didn't matter. Well, it mattered a bit, but it was hardly the end of their relationship. It was just one aspect that would need work. After all, he'd been just as gentle, courteous and kind as a girl could have asked of a man going at it for the first time, with her at any rate, although she'd not thought to ask if he was a virgin. However, if he was, it would have explained a lot. And with that in her mind as she lay there, she decided to buy him a copy of the latest instructional relationship DVD called *Cum in 20*, which promised to teach men how to take a girl to heaven and back in just twenty minutes, without the use of either an aeroplane or the services of a spiritual medium.

Whilst Abigail's brain ambled down towards the YouGet store in town that she thought would sell *Cum in 20*, and that she may as well pick herself up a copy of *Fit in 15* at the same time, Will, meanwhile, was feeling rather pleased with himself.

About an hour earlier, as they'd made their way into

121

her flat, and then the kitchen, not only had he been able to avoid any further discussion about the film *Three Hundred and Sixty Five Dresses,* so she hadn't discovered that he'd slept through the whole thing, but he'd been able to instigate a snogging session even before the kettle had boiled. And once he'd been manhandled into her bedroom, just across the hall, he'd been fortunate enough to have sex with her, twice! And not only that, but he'd even been able to disguise the fact that he'd prematurely ejaculated when she was helping him to put the first condom on, a potentially embarrassing situation he'd managed to cover up by saying that the prophylactic's micro-fibres must have become misaligned, forcing him to have a go with another. And on top of all that, he'd still been able to prevent her from finding out his deepest, darkest secret, that *he* was the child she'd gone to school with all those years ago, who she used to call Wee Willy Wankett, the boy who never seemed to be able to find his blankett.

And as he lay in Abigail's bed, staring up at her ceiling, he did a quick mental count of all the girls he'd managed to have sex with so far. Three! But with Abigail, that made four!

He smiled to himself. *Four girls! Not bad,* he thought. *Not great, but not bad, considering I've been lumbered with the name Richard Will bloody Wankett!*

From out of the bedroom's quite darkness came the sound of Abigail's mobile phone, on the floor somewhere amongst all the clothes she'd discarded on her way onto the bed.

'Not now!' she said, as she snuggled up closer to

the warmth of Will's lean naked body.

The phone soon stopped ringing, but only to start up a moment or two later.

'Crap,' she said. 'It must be Eliot. I can't imagine anyone else calling twice like that. I'd better take it.'

'Do you have to?' asked Will. If it was his phone ringing at such a time, he'd have most definitely ignored it.

'I'd better.' She dragged herself to the edge of the bed, and without getting out, reached for her jeans where she thought her phone should be. It was there. She was also right about who the caller was, and managed to answer it before it rang off.

'Abigail Love speaking.'

'Abigail, hi, it's Eliot.'

'Oh, hello, Eliot,' she said, feigning surprise.

'Listen. A huge story's just broken. The local Conservative MP has just been found by police at his house, tied up in full bondage gear with his wife. They'd both being enjoying the many attentions of not one, but two male escorts. Is there any chance you could get down there? I know it's a big ask, but you're the only person I've been able to get hold of.'

It did sound like a great story, but she was in bed, naked, having just had sex for the first time with someone she now considered to be her brand new boyfriend. And as career-minded as she was, she felt that leaving her bed at such a time was above and beyond the call of duty.

'I'm really sorry, Eliot, but I've already turned in for the night.'

'Look, I'll make it worth your while, I promise!'

Abigail paused for a moment, before asking, 'Where is it?'

'6, Hellene Road, just off Eastern Parade,' said Eliot, and out of desperation, added, 'I'll even give you a bonus if you go!'

'You'll give me a bonus?'

'If you cover the story, yes!'

'How much?' she asked, just in case his idea of a bonus was dramatically different from hers.

'Oh, er…' When Eliot had picked up the phone to call her, he'd not expected to have to offer her money to convince her to take the story. 'How about £50?'

'If you make it £500, I'll be down there within half an hour.'

'Deal!' agreed Eliot.

He knew it was too much, but if this story was the result of McDongle's promise to him, as he hoped it was, then the man was as good as his word, and there was subsequently a good chance that more stories would follow, and he'd just have to plan ahead to make sure he didn't have to keep forking out bonuses each time they did.

'Can you try and get hold of Will?' he asked. There was no way he was going to be able to offer him a pay rise as well, but hoped that, by now, Abigail would have enough of a hold on him to persuade him to attend without one.

'Oh, yes,' she answered, glancing around at Will who was still lying next to her, and looking as if he was listening to their conversation, well, half of it at least. 'I'm sure that I'll be able to get hold of him,' she answered. She'd done so earlier, three times in fact, so she didn't think it would be too difficult to do it again.

'Great. Thanks, Abigail.'

'OK, no problem. Bye for now.'

Hanging up, she said to Will, 'I'm sorry darling, but we need to get down to Hellene Road.'

You must be fucking joking, he thought, but with great mental restraint, said instead, 'Of course, no problem at all.'

'I don't suppose you can call a cab, while I sort my face out?'

'Sure,' and he dragged himself out of bed and joined what he hoped was now his new girlfriend, as they started to pick through the clothes on the floor, trying to identify which items belonged to whom.

When they'd both managed to get dressed, and Abigail had sat down at her dressing table to busy herself with her hair and makeup, both of which were in need of some urgent attention, Will asked, 'Have you got any taxi numbers knocking about somewhere?'

'There are some of their business cards out in the hall, in the drawer under the phone,' she said, as she began re-applying her mascara.

It was only a small one-bedroom flat, so it didn't take long for Will to find both the hall and the landline phone that was in it. And sure enough, there were several taxi company business cards in the drawer, along with numerous menus. Selecting a cab firm he recognised, he lifted the phone and dialled the number.

'Captain Cabs?' came a man's voice from the other end.

'Yes, hello. Can I order a cab, please?'

'When for?'

'As soon as possible.'

'What's the address?'

'Oh yes, of course. Hold on,' and covering the mouthpiece, he called out, 'Abi, what's the address here?'

'Flat 4, 12, St Vincent Street,' she called back.

Returning to the call, he said, 'It's Flat 4, 12, St Vincent Street.'

'And what's the name?'

'It's Wankett. Will Wankett.'

'Wankett?' asked the man.

'Yes, that's right. Wankett,' he replied. He always hated having to give out his surname.

'OK. We should have one over to you in about ten minutes.'

'Great, thanks.' He set the receiver back into the cradle.

Then he froze, just like someone starting a Mannequin Challenge.

He'd said his surname. He'd said his surname, and he'd said it out loud. He'd said his surname, he'd said it out loud, and Abigail Love, his nemesis from school, known to him then as Fanny-Gail the Horrible, his most bitter playground rival, and the girl he'd just had sex with, twice, was in the bedroom opposite. And the door was still open!

SHIT! he thought. *SHIT, SHIT, SHIT, SHIT, SHIT, SHIT, SHIT*, he thought again. *But hold on. How loudly did I say it?* his mind asked itself. *I had to speak quite loudly when I asked her for the address. Yes, I did. I had to almost shout. And she had to almost shout back. She probably didn't hear. She might have done, but she probably didn't. Fuck it. I'm just going to have to sneak back into her bedroom and take a look. If she standing there, all ready to start a rendition of, 'Oh look, it's Wee Willy Wankett,' before asking me if I'd ever been able to find my blankett, then I'll know that she did, and it's just game over. It's not life over, it's just game over, and I'll have to move back in with my Mum and find another job somewhere. But she may not have done! Fuck it!*

With the caution of an assassin who'd just entered the premises of his next target, Will tiptoed back towards the bedroom door and ever so slowly poked his head around the corner.

She was still sitting at her dressing table, staring at herself in the mirror.

Gulping, he announced, 'I've called a cab!'

She didn't respond.

'They should be here in about ten minutes,' he continued.

'I'll be with you in a sec,' she replied, clearly pre-occupied. And as she replaced the lid of her lipstick and began to prod at her hair, she asked, 'Have you got your iPhone?

She hadn't heard. She would have said something if she had, surely?

'Er, yes, I have,' he answered, as he checked to make sure that he did.

Standing up, she smiled at him, and asked, 'How do I look?'

She hadn't heard, he repeated to himself, and with huge relief, said, 'You look absolutely fantastic!'

CHAPTER TWENTY ONE
A STICKY SITUATION

TURNING IN TO Hellene Road, it was fairly obvious that they hadn't beaten the police to it, not by a long way, as the entire street seemed to be lit up by blue flashing lights.

'You can drop us off here, please,' said Abigail to the cab driver.

'Right you are, miss,' the cabbie replied, and pulled over to one side of the quiet suburban street to glance down at his meter. 'That'll be £25.'

Pulling the correct amount from her purse, Abi handed a couple of notes over to him, saying, 'Here you go.' She returned her purse to her handbag, pushed open the door, and stepped out, with Will following behind.

As they made their way towards where the focus of police activity seemed to be, Abi briefed Will as to how they were going to approach the story. 'I suggest we make use of the fact that you don't have a big camera again, and try walking straight in through the front door.'

By that time they'd already reached the POLICE DO NOT CROSS tape, and Will simply nodded his agreement and held the tape up for both of them to duck under. He followed her as she marched across the driveway towards the front door of the property, where a policeman stood guard.

Taking her press pass out from her handbag, she

held it up for the constable to see and endeavoured to walk straight past. But just as she thought she was about to get by, the strong arm of the law intervened, the one belonging to the policeman, which he stuck out to physically stop her from going any further.

'I'm sorry, miss,' he said, without looking down at her, 'but it's police personnel only, I'm afraid.'

'How dare you! I *am* the police!' she announced, and gave the man a very hard stare.

The constable turned his head slowly, engaged eye contact, and without warning, snatched her ID out of her hand and began to examine it.

'It says here that you're from *Hampshire Today*?' he asked.

'Yes, that's correct,' she agreed. And hoping that he'd yet to hear about them, being that they were still relatively new, added, 'We're the Special Police Communications Squad!'

As he brought the card into the light coming from the house to have a better look, he asked, 'What does the "Press Pass" bit mean then?'

'Oh, that!' she said, and after her brain had had a chance to come up with some sort of plausible answer, said, 'It just means that we have authority to, er, get past the press. You know, like when they're in our way.'

'I see. And what about him then?' the policeman asked, looking behind her at Will, who was doing his very best to look nothing like a journalist.

'He's with me.'

'Can I see your ID, please?' asked the constable, staring at Will.

Will hadn't been given his Hampshire Today press pass yet, and doubted if his Instathon credit card would do the trick. Probably the best he could come up with was a library card, but that was out of date. So, instead of showing him anything, he thought he'd have a go at making something up, like his new girlfriend seemed to be rather good at doing.

'I can't do that, I'm afraid,' he said.

'And why's that?'

'I'm working undercover.'

'For this Hampshire Today thing?'

'That's right!' said Will, looking straight at the police constable. 'I'm a special undercover police man person,' he said, delighted with himself for being able to come up with something from off the top of his head.

Before the police constable had a chance to put two and two together to come up with anything other than five, Abigail asked, 'Are forensics here yet?'

'Well, yes, they're inside, but…'

'And who's in charge?'

'That would be Detective Inspector Hardwick.'

'Right! Then we'd better have a word with him, hadn't we!' She snatched her press pass from out of the police constable's hand, and she and Will barged straight past him to take the steps up to the open front door two at a time.

Once inside, Abigail stopped. To be honest, she hadn't expected to get so far, not through the front door at any rate, and now that they were standing in the posh hallway, with its magnolia walls, cream coloured carpets and a sparkling chandelier hanging from the stairwell, she'd no idea what to do, or where to go.

Sensing her quandary, Will suggested, 'Maybe we should try and find this Hardwick character, and see if he can tell us what happened?'

Not too keen to let on that she hadn't thought of that, she asked, 'Yes, but which way?'

They both stopped to listen, but the house seemed perfectly still. Then they heard something move upstairs.

'They must be up in one of the bedrooms,' surmised Will.

Abigail nodded her agreement, and led the way up the softly-carpeted stairs.

Reaching the first floor landing, she stopped again, listened for a moment, and then turned right into a spacious bedroom, featuring another chandelier with an unmade double bed underneath.

Crawling around on the floor were two people wearing white overalls, and in the corner was a young-looking sandy-haired man in a dark blue suit, staring at a small black notebook.

'Excuse me?' asked Abigail, 'Are you Detective Inspector Hardwick?'

Looking up in surprise, the man said, 'Er, no. I'm Sergeant Dewbush. Hardwick's in the toilet.'

'My name's Abigail, and this is my colleague, Will. We're from Hampshire Today Special Police Communications Squad,' she announced, as she flashed her press pass at him. 'Would you mind telling us what happened here?'

'Ah, yes, of course. Well, when we arrived...'

'Is it OK if we record this?' she interrupted, as she took the opportunity to retrieve her microphone from out of her handbag.

'Oh, well, er. It's, um, not—' said the young sergeant.

'It's just to make sure we don't miss anything,' explained Abigail.

As the sergeant had never met anyone from a special police communications squad before, he could only assume that it was standard practice for them, so he said, 'Well, OK, I suppose.'

'Great!' and holding up her microphone she turned to Will and said, 'This is Abigail Love reporting from inside the house of Conservative MP, Michael Brownfield. Here with me is Sergeant Bushdew, of the Solent Police.'

She turned to look at the policeman and asked, 'Sergeant Bushdew, can you tell us exactly what took place here?'

'It's actually Dew*bush*,' corrected the sergeant, switching his gaze from the microphone which Abigail held up to his mouth to the iPhone that Will was using to film him.

'Yes, of course, sorry. Can you tell us what happened, Sergeant Dewbush?'

'Um, well, er, yes. We received an anonymous call that the house had been broken into, and that the occupants were being tortured and raped.'

'Tortured *and* raped?' asked Abigail, for dramatic effect.

'Yes, that's right.'

'And what did you find when you arrived?'

'There was no answer to the door, but there was a light on in the upstairs bedroom, from where we could hear noises.'

'What sort of noises?'

'Well, they didn't sound like those inside were having a great time. More like several people experiencing considerable pain. So we broke down the door and rushed up here where we found…'

But the sergeant had stopped talking, and stared over at the bed with a wistful expression, as if re-living the moment.

'So? What did you find?' urged Abigail.

'Well, um. When we came in here, to this room, there were two people, a man and a woman, gagged and tied to the bed, face down, who were both wearing this black and red bondage type gear. And on top of them were two really large men.'

The young sergeant had stopped again, and although she felt she already knew the answer, Abigail asked, 'And what were they doing?'

'They seemed to be in the most dreadful pain.'

'The two underneath?'

'No, the two men on top.'

'What about the couple underneath?'

'We weren't sure about them. They both had these red ball type things strapped to their mouths, so they could have been in pain, or they could have been enjoying it. It was difficult to tell, but the two on top were shouting and screaming, and kept pointing at their, er, thingies. So it was fairly obvious that something was wrong. But when we tried to pull them off, they screamed even more. And it soon became apparent that they were stuck!'

'Stuck?'

'Yes, stuck!'

'What, both of them?'

'Uh-huh. And after they'd been taken away in a couple of ambulances, we found an empty tube of superglue in one of the drawers, alongside some K-Y Jelly. It looks like they'd mixed them together before, er, getting down to it.'

'But why on earth would they have done that?'

'I've no idea. My boss says that we're going to have to conduct a full investigation, but not until they're all out of intensive care, but at this stage he says that it could be foul play.'

In complete shock herself, and before anyone cottoned on to the fact that they weren't police, but journalists, Abigail turned to look around at Will's camera. 'Well, there you have it!' she began. 'The Conservative MP, Michael Brownfield, likes having other men stick themselves up his bum, literally! And so it would appear does his wife. This is Abigail Love, reporting for Hampshire Today. Back to the studio.'

CHAPTER TWENTY TWO
CHILDHOOD MEMORIES

THE FOLLOWING afternoon, with her latest story leading Hampshire Today's news once again, Abigail took a long lunch break to catch up with a girl she'd known since school: her best friend, Sally Davies, who was now a senior negotiator for a local estate agency.

But this meeting wasn't just to tell her about her recent success at work. It was far more important than that. Since the evening before, when Will had ordered that cab, she'd been desperate to talk to someone, because, despite pretending that she hadn't, she *had* heard Will give his surname out over the phone, and she was now in urgent need of a friendly chat.

As they sat down with their Skinny Lattes and Coffeebean's famous Low Fat Cucumber & Cottage Cheese sandwiches, Abigail said to Sally, 'I need your advice.'

'You need *my* advice?'

'I know it's rare, but yes.'

'Are you sure about that?' asked her best friend. 'The last time you asked me for my advice you made a point of declaring that you'd never be asking me again.'

'I know.'

'*Ever!*' re-iterated Sally.

'Yes, but in fairness, that was because you told me

to dye my hair blue.'

'I seem to remember that you were trying to attract the attention of a Chelsea football supporter. And besides, it's not my fault that you thought I meant your *hair* hair.'

'But who in their right mind would tell someone to dye their hair blue, without making it clear that they were referring to their pubes?'

Sally just shrugged. 'You were lucky that blue hair suited you.'

'Blue hair doesn't suit anyone.'

'My gran's got blue hair, and I think she looks great.'

'Apart from women in their eighties, but that's not what I wanted to talk to you about.'

'What happened between you and Gary, anyway?'

'As I said, I don't want to talk about it!'

'I take it he didn't like blue hair then?'

Abigail scowled at her.

'OK, so what's on your mind, apart from hair colour and opportunities lost?'

Picking up her coffee, Abigail took a tentative sip, before asking, 'You know school?'

'Our school, or schools in general?'

'Our one.'

'Er, yes. I think so. What about it?'

'Do you remember a certain boy there?'

'One in particular? I seem to remember there were quite a few, and I only had so much time.'

'I've never asked you this Sally, but just exactly how many boys *did* you have sex with at school?'

'Only the ones I fancied.'

'And what about the rest? I suppose they just got a blow job as some sort of consolation prize.'

'Oh please! I gave *hand jobs* out as consolation prizes. I saved the blow jobs for the teachers. But still, good times though,' said Sally, as she gazed off into space with a nostalgic smile.

'You were just *such* a slut back then.' said Abigail.

'I thought I still was? Anyway, you can talk!'

'Yes, I *can* talk, thank you very much. You should try it sometime, especially when it comes to chatting up men, and preferably before asking if they'd like to play with your tits.'

'I only asked that once!'

'Once? That was your chat up line!'

'Maybe. But it worked though,' and just before taking a sip from her coffee, she whispered half to herself, '*Still does.*'

'Anyway,' said Abigail, choosing to ignore that last remark, 'apart from discussing just how much of a slut you are, and how big your tits were—'

'*Still are,*' she interrupted, but again to herself.

'—I need to try and focus your over-sexed brain on just one boy, and one who was in our class.'

Sally put her hands to her temples in preparation for deep meditative thought, closed her eyes and said, 'Ready!'

'Are you sure?'

'Not really,' and she gave up. 'I need some sort of a thinking cap. I don't suppose I can pop out and buy one? I saw this really cute little beret in Oasis on the way here, and it was only £20.'

'Oh do shut up! There was this one boy in our

class…'

'You just said that. What was his name?'

'It was, er, Will.'

'Will?'

'Yes, Will. Will Wankett.'

'You mean Wee Willy Wankett? The boy without a blankett?' and Sally burst into fits of hysterics at the memory.

However, when she realised that Abigail wasn't joining in, but was instead staring at her with all the seriousness of someone trying to decide which earrings to wear, she stopped, and after a moment's pause, asked, 'He's not dead, is he?'

'No. It's worse than that, I'm afraid.'

'Don't tell me he's been on X Factor?'

'NO!'

'Well, what about him then?' asked Sally, taking another sip from her coffee.

'He's my boyfriend.'

Sally sprayed her coffee all over Abigail's Low Fat Cucumber & Cottage Cheese sandwich.

'Gee, thanks Sally. I knew my sandwich needed a little something, and now I know what it was. Your coffee, spat out all over it. Nice!'

'Sorry about that,' said Sally, horrified by what she'd done, and as she picked up her paper napkin to begin dabbing at her best friend's sandwich, said in her defence, 'but you should've given me a warning before telling me something like that.'

'Yes, well, I didn't know how else to say it.'

'So it's true then? You are going out with…*him*?'

'I think so, yes.'

'How do you mean, you think so?'

'Well, we only had sex for the first time last night, but I didn't know who he was then.'

'And you call *me* a tart?'

'I mean, I knew who he was, of course, but I just didn't know that he was Will Wankett, from school. He only joined us at work on Monday. I must admit that I thought I recognised him, but I'd not seen him since we left, and he's changed a fair bit since then.'

'But you must have recognised his surname, surely?'

'That's just it. I didn't know what it was! And it was only when I heard him ordering a cab last night, *after* we'd had sex, that the penny dropped, and I realised that I'd just slept with the boy I used to tease at school.

'I see,' said Sally, endeavouring to express empathy. 'And after he'd called the cab, and you found out that it was Will Wankett, did you get a chance to ask him if he'd ever been able to find his blankett?' she asked, supressing a smirk.

'*This is serious!*'

'No kidding!' Sally agreed. 'A Wankett without a blankett? It doesn't get much more serious than that!'

'Yes, all right. Ha! Ha! Very funny! So now that you know who it is, what am I going to do?'

'Er, what, you mean apart from trying to find him something soft and warm for Christmas, to go on top of his bed?'

Abigail gave her a very hard stare.

'Sorry. So…anyway, he *must* know who you are?'

'That's the problem. I don't know!'

'But he knows your surname?'

'I think so.'

'Then he knows who you are! There can't be two Abigail Loves, not this side of London.'

'But he hasn't said anything. I'd have thought he would have at least asked about it by now, if he'd known. So, I was thinking that he may not remember who I was.'

'Do you honestly think he wouldn't remember you?'

'Maybe,' said Abigail, but without much conviction.

'You do realise that you made that boy's life a living hell, and from the moment he sat down in class.'

'Well yes, but only when I found out what his surname was.'

'Which was at registration, at 9am, on the very first day. And that's when you stood up, right in the middle of the class, and called out, 'Look everyone, it's Wee Willy Wankett!' whilst pointing at him and laughing.

'*I did not!*' said Abigail, appalled at the very idea.

'I'm fairly sure you did. And that's when you asked him if he'd lost his blankett. Don't get me wrong Abi, it was really funny, but you just didn't let up, and kept saying it over and over again every time you saw him, and for the next five years.'

'You're probably right.'

'There's no probably about it, and that's why he'll definitely remember you.'

'Yes, but if that's the case, why hasn't he said anything?'

'I've no idea. Maybe he's managed to block it from his memory through a course of self-hypnosis? I must admit that I did hear a rumour that he'd started seeing a child psychiatrist. Maybe they managed to convince him that it wasn't happening, and it was all in his imagination?'

'You never told me he was seeing a psychiatrist.'

'No? Well, I probably thought that if you knew that he was going through the process of losing his marbles, you'd have started to ask him if he needed help finding them, which he probably wouldn't have appreciated.'

Ignoring her again, Abigail said, 'So, anyway…what do you think I should do?'

'About what, his marbles or his blankett?'

'About going out with him?'

'You're not seriously suggesting that you're going to continue to see him, knowing that the very moment he finds out who you really are, he'll probably come at you with a knife.'

'He wouldn't do that, would he?'

'No, you're right. He wouldn't. He'd use an axe instead.'

'This really isn't helping, Sally.'

'Look, Abi, I'm just saying, as your friend, you were *really* mean to him, and for a *really* long time.'

'Yes, I know. But I only did it because I liked him.'

'You only did it because you…what?'

'Because I liked him.'

'Seriously?'

Abigail nodded.

'You dragged that poor boy through hell and back for five long years because you fancied him?'

She nodded again. 'I know it sounds stupid, but I didn't know what else I could do to let him know how

I felt.'

'You could have stuck your tongue down his throat for a start. At least that would have given him some sort of an idea.'

Abigail couldn't help herself, and let out a laugh.

'I take it you still like him then?' asked Sally.

'I'm afraid so.'

'A little, or a lot?'

'Unfortunately, rather a lot.'

Their table fell silent.

'Then you've got no choice. If he doesn't already know, then you're just going to have to tell him, aren't you?'

'Yes, I know. But how?'

'Maybe you could buy him a blanket and sew his name on it? Then you could take it around to him and say that you'd found it.'

'That's about as stupid as advising me to dye my hair blue.'

'You're the one who keeps asking for my advice. Anyway, you have a little think about it, and I'll go and get you another sandwich.'

CHAPTER TWENTY THREE
HYPNOTISM UNMASKED

JUST AFTER lunch, McDongle popped around for a meeting with his election agent, Elizabeth Potts, to chat about how things had gone the evening before, and to discuss the next phase of his plan to become a Member of Parliament.

'I hear that the old superglue-in-the-K-Y Jelly idea worked then?' asked Elizabeth, as she brought two coffees in to her dining room office where McDongle had already made himself comfortable.

'Oh yes,' said McDongle, taking the steaming hot mug from her. 'There was little doubt about that. You should have seen the look on everyone's faces when they all realised they were stuck together. Especially those Eastern European chaps I hired. Actually, you *can* if you like. I posted the film of it onto YouTube this morning.'

'Maybe later,' said Elizabeth. She did want to see it, of course, but she had another client coming at three.

'I saw that Hampshire Today gave you a mention,' she continued. 'They said that you were the one who uncovered Michael Brownfield's passion for bondage, and having well-endowed men shag him up the bum.'

'They didn't say it quite like that, I hope?' asked McDongle, who'd yet to watch the news that day.

'Probably not, but they said enough to give people the gist.'

'Did they mention that his wife shared similar

143

interests?'

'Oh yes! They were both heavily featured in the story. They even showed a picture of them from their wedding.'

Taking her first sip of coffee, she asked, 'So, am I right in assuming that Hampshire Today did agree to support your campaign in exchange for some half-decent news stories?'

'They did, and it sounds like they're keeping to their side of the bargain.'

'Good!' She took another sip from her coffee, and moved the conversation on. 'Anyway, a by-election's already been called, so now we just need to worry about the candidate that Labour are putting forward, a certain Mr Harold Webber,' and she reached over the table to pick up a red election leaflet that had come through her door earlier that day.

'I've been thinking about that,' said McDongle, as he took it from her and glanced down at it. 'I thought that maybe we could simply plant some kind of recreational drugs on him, like heroine, or cocaine, and then let the police know. As long as it was only enough for personal use, they wouldn't lock him up for it, but I'd have thought that it would cast a big enough shadow over his campaign for him not to be a threat.'

'But would it though?' asked Elizabeth, as she put her mug down and folded her arms to gaze up at the corner of the room. 'I'm not sure that it would. I think most people these days just assume MP's are on drugs, legally or otherwise.'

'How about we link him with something to do with children?' suggested McDongle.

'It's too risky. We need him to stand, and just the mention of the word "paedophile" during a campaign is enough for the candidate in question to be forced to stand down.'

Regretting he hadn't been told that before dealing with Michael Brownfield, McDongle asked, 'But would it matter if he didn't stand though? Surely, it would only serve to benefit my campaign if he was locked up?'

'With UKIP doing so well at the moment, I think it would be safer to have him around,' said Elizabeth. 'If he doesn't stand, then all his supporters will simply jump ship, but it won't be our ship they'd be jumping to. No. We need him, but somehow to make it look like you're a better option.'

They both fell silent, as they mulled over the problem.

After another sip from her coffee, Elizabeth said, 'Ideally, what would work best would be if he came over to the electorate as being even more right wing than your average Conservative. That way, his Labour voters would swing right, but only enough to vote for you, instead of him.'

Silence fell again, before McDongle suggested, 'How about if we could make him out to be some sort of closet Nazi type?' He didn't know much about politics, not really, but he did at least know that the Nazi party was just about as right wing as it was possible to go, without eradicating the human species.

'That's not a bad idea,' said Elizabeth, as she leant forward to pick up a biro and start taking notes. 'We could send a story over to Hampshire Today that he's got a picture of Adolf Hitler on his bedroom wall. And maybe say that he collects Nazi memorabilia, and that he follows Alt-Right on Twitter.'

'And his name does sound a little Germanic,' added McDongle. 'Couldn't we also mention that his family originated from Germany, and that his father was in the SS?'

'Yes, and I've thought of something else as well!' exclaimed Elizabeth, clearly enjoying the creative process. 'Have you heard of a chap called Magic Malcolm?'

'No, I don't think so,' said McDongle, but he couldn't be sure. 'Is he some sort of Neo-Nazi strippergram?'

'No, nothing like that. He's a mesmerist. You know, one of those performers who hypnotises people on stage, and makes them do stupid things.'

'OK, well yes. I know what you mean. Go on,' he prompted, unsure where his agent was going with this.

'I did a fair bit of work for him a while back, and he owes me a favour or two. I bet he could hypnotise Harold Webber into believing that he actually *was* a Neo Nazi! And if he could, then it would certainly give a new slant to his campaign speeches.'

As she wrote the idea down, she added, 'And he may even be able to make him do a Nazi salute, whenever anyone either said or did something.'

A broad white grin spread over McDongle's huge fat orange face. 'Now I *do* like that,' he said. 'I like that a lot!'

And with a plan of action agreed, Elizabeth Potts opened up her CRM database to dig out Magic

Malcolm's phone number.

CHAPTER TWENTY FOUR
NICE DAY FOR IT

AFTER RETURNING from her lunch with Sally, and seeing the man who was apparently her boyfriend, Wee Willy Wankett, sitting on his own across the desk from hers, looking lonely, she made a concerted effort to be super-nice to him for what was left of the afternoon. And when the clock reached five, she asked if he'd like to come out for a drink with her after work. She knew that if she really was going to reveal her true identity to him, face-to-face, then she was going to need at least one drink, but more likely three.

'What would you like?' she asked, once they'd reached the bar of the Badger & Hamster pub.

The venue had been her choice, as it was always crowded, and she felt it was going to be less likely that he'd make a scene after she told him if there were lots of other people around. She also considered that it was safer than a restaurant, as there was no cutlery for him to attack her with. 'My treat,' she added, in a bid to keep his mood buoyant.

'Could I have a pint of Portsmouth Pride?' he asked.

'Sure, no problemo.'

She didn't normally go around saying "no problemo" all the time, but she would have been the first to admit that she was nervous.

Catching the barman's eye, she asked, 'A pint of Portsmouth Pride and a Bacardi & Coke, please,' but glancing at Will, changed her mind and called after the barman, 'Sorry, could you make that a double?'

As soon as their drinks arrived on the bar top, she lifted her glass, said, 'Cheers,' before gulping down the entire contents, and her empty glass was back down on the bar before Will had even a chance to pick his up.

Although he'd never seen her drink quite so quickly, and had certainly never heard her use such a lame phrase as "no problemo", Will assumed that she was simply gearing up to ask him back to her place again, and with that in mind, asked, 'Can I get you another?'

'Thank you, Will. Yes please.'

A few minutes later, with drinks in hand, Abigail led Will to a quiet corner where she spent a few moments checking out all the main points of exit, just in case she needed to make a run for it.

Sitting down, she said, 'This is nice,' smiling at Will, as he made himself comfortable opposite her.

'I think it's my favourite pub in Portsmouth,' he said, happy to go along with making small talk for a while.

'And the weather certainly is very pleasant, for the time of year,' added Abigail, as they both looked out the window to see that it had just started raining.

'Yes, very,' said Will, keen not to enter into a disagreement about the weather.

'So, here we are then!' continued Abigail, giving Will an exaggerated smile.

But by now Will had sensed something wasn't right.

He'd been in this situation before, and it was normally just before being dumped.

'Are you OK?' he asked. 'You seem a little…preoccupied.'

'Do I?' she said, taking the opportunity to drain the contents of her glass again.

'A little, yes.'

'Would you like another?' she asked, looking at the pint that he'd yet to even start.

'I'm fine, thank you.'

Abigail stared into his dreamy brown eyes and wished she'd taken Sally's advice and bought him a blanket with his name on it instead. Now that the time had come, she'd no idea how she was going to break it to him that she was the girl at school who'd made his life so miserable.

'Did I ever ask you what your favourite colour is?' she asked, in a desperate bid to buy herself more time.

'I'm fairly sure you did. It was when we were here before.'

'Oh yes, that's right. What was it again?'

'Blue.'

'Blue. Yes of course. Good choice! And you're a Capricorn, aren't you?'

'Uh-huh.'

'I'm a Pisces.'

'I know.'

Will took his first sip from his pint as he continued to stare at her. If she was going to dump him, then he was buggered if he was going to make it easy for her.

Taking a deep breath, Abigail gulped, and said, 'Will, I, er, I have a confession to make.'

She's seeing someone else, he thought. *Either that or she's a divorcee with three children. No, she's too young, surely. Maybe she's a shopaholic and is massively in debt. Or she could be a lesbian, of course.*

'We've, er, actually met before,' she continued, and stared down at her empty glass.

Will's heart thudded hard in his chest, and he could feel his face begin to flush.

She's found out! he thought. *She must have done!*

As his entire body felt like it had begun to play pinball with itself, but at ten times the normal speed, he carefully rested his pint down on the table and asked, just as casually as it was possible for him to, under the circumstances, 'We have?'

'You went to Whitworth School, in Gosport, right?'

She knew! She fucking knew! He thought, as the pinball gamed exploded into something more like nuclear paintball.

But why is she still being so nice to me? he asked himself. *In fact, why hasn't she stood up on her chair and started shouting, 'Look everyone, it's Wee Willy Wankett' before asking if I'd ever managed to find my blankett?'*

With all the trepidation of a man entering a lion's cage armed only with a tin of cat food, he said, 'That's correct.'

But as soon as he'd admitted to it, a new realisation dawned on him. Somehow she had found out, and yet she'd neither dumped him on the spot, which was what he thought she would have done, nor had she taken the opportunity to pick up where she'd left off at school, by sending out an email to everyone at work asking them to keep an eye out for a blankett belonging to their new cameraman, Mr Richard Will Wankett. *So, if she knows but hasn't already dumped me,* he thought, *or re-commenced my public torture, then that must mean that she still…likes me? Is that possible?*

'I was in your class.' she continued. 'Abigail Love. Don't you remember me?' she asked, looking at him from the most beautiful eyes imaginable.

It was possible, he thought.

Having come to that realisation, with sudden and deep regret he realised that he was still completely and utterly screwed. He'd known exactly who she was from the first day they'd met, but had deliberately not mentioned it, and the second she found out that he'd been lying to her all this time, that would be it!

So as paintball turned back to pinball, his brain mentally bounced between the two choices he seemed to be faced with, neither one he particularly liked. To either admit that he'd always known who she was, but had deliberately kept it from her, or to lie again and pretend that he'd never seen her before in his life, at least not since Monday.

He could feel the seconds tick by, and she was now staring at him, with the clear expectation for some sort of an answer.

He had to make a choice, and he had to do it now, because the answer to her question, 'Don't you remember me?' would take him down a road it would be difficult to get off, not without ploughing straight into oncoming traffic.

'I'm sorry, but I'm not sure I do,' he eventually answered.

'Oh!' she said, taken completely by surprise. She

wasn't expecting that, and was now almost offended. 'Are you sure?' she asked. 'I used to wear really awful glasses, and wore my hair like this,' and as she said that, she pulled her hair back into a makeshift ponytail.

It worked, and apart from the lack of glasses, it was as if the girl he'd always known as Fanny Gail the Horrible was sitting directly opposite him, grinning, but wearing eyeshadow and mascara, and with the most sumptuous red lips.

'No, sorry,' he said, now adamant that he couldn't admit to having known her; and then he thought that he really should do something to try and make her suffer for all those years of psychological torment. So he asked, 'Why, should I?'

She brought her hair back down and stared at her drink.

'Well, possibly. I used to tease you a bit. That was all.'

Pretending to be shocked, he said, 'Really! What did you used to say?'

'Oh, something stupid, no doubt.'

'Go on, tell me?' he asked

But Abigail was now seriously wishing that she'd never brought the subject up.

'I really can't remember,' she said, unable to look at him in the eyes.

Now that they were discussing it, even if not directly, Will was becoming increasingly intent on exacting some sort of revenge.

'But surely, if you can remember me, and that you used to tease me, then you must remember what you used to say?'

'No, honestly, Will, I can't.'

'Perhaps it had something to do with my surname,' he asked, as he took sadistic pleasure in watching her squirm.

'I really can't,' she said, desperate for the conversation to end. 'It was all just such a long time ago.'

'You know what my surname is, I assume?' he continued, unwilling to let it go.

'Well, yes, of course I know what your surname is.'

'And it has nothing to do with that?'

'I can't remember, I promise!'

Abigail could feel herself about to burst into tears, and her fragile emotional state wasn't being helped by the fact that she'd realised that if he couldn't remember her, then he'd never felt the same about her at school as she had done, and still did!

Will could tell that she was about to cry, and the moment he realised, he stopped. There was just no way that he'd be able to hurt her. Not with such malicious intent. It simply wasn't in his nature.

However, the previously buried memories that the conversation had brought to the surface had left him seriously pissed off with her, and now at himself as well, for having stopped short of forcing her to repeat, there and then, that immortal phrase. He knew that could have been his long dreamt-of chance for retaliation, and he'd let her off!

They sat in silence for a few moments, with the only sounds coming from Abigail as she drummed her nails on her empty glass, and Will as he started to drink his pint just as quickly as possible.

After a while, Abigail sniffed, and with remarkable volume considering how small her nose was. She began to rummage around in her handbag for a tissue, and asked, 'Would you like to come back to my place?' hoping for the opportunity to be able to start making up for all those years of psychological abuse.

Obviously Will would have liked nothing more than to have sex with her again. He was, after all, a heterosexual man, and she a woman he found devastatingly attractive. But he was still fuming with the resurfaced memories of his school days, and simply wouldn't allow himself.

'I can't tonight. Sorry,' he said, without sounding sorry at all.

Abigail's shoulders slumped, visibly.

Knocking back the remains of his pint, he glanced at his watch, saying, 'Anyway, I've got a few things to do,' as he stood up. He then put his empty pint down on the table, said, 'See you later,' and just walked out.

'That went well,' said Abigail, out loud to herself, and after turning around to make sure that he really had gone, and wasn't going to change his mind and come back to her, she returned to her handbag to dig out her phone. Although she was holding her best friend, Sally bloody Davies, directly responsible for ruining her evening, and quite possibly the rest of her life, nonetheless, she was desperate to tell her what had happened.

CHAPTER TWENTY FIVE
TRACKS AND TRAINS

THE FOLLOWING morning, Elizabeth arranged for McDongle and herself to meet Magic Malcolm - known off-stage as Malcolm Grange - outside the house of Mr Harold Webber, the Labour candidate who'd been put forward for the recently announced Portsmouth and Gosport by-election.

She'd already briefed Malcolm on the phone as to what they wanted him to do, and although he wasn't too thrilled by the prospect of allowing himself to become embroiled in something that sounded distinctly dodgy, the offer of £500, which was more than he'd make from one of his shows, and the promise that his involvement would be kept a firm secret, was enough to persuade him to attend.

As the rain that hadn't stopped since the evening before continued to pour down, the three people huddled underneath their respective umbrellas as Elizabeth made the introductions.

'Malcolm Grange, this is Douglas McDongle. He'll be helping us out with our little job today.'

The two men shook hands and mumbled, 'Hello' to each other.

'This is where the man we'd like you to hypnotise lives,' she said, pointing at the large white detached house opposite where they stood. 'Again, his name is Harold Webber, and he's unmarried, so he should be on his own.'

'That's all fine,' said Malcolm, 'but we're going to have to get him inside and make him feel relaxed. I won't be able to do it out on the porch.'

'Don't worry, we've already thought of that. We've found out that he's a model railway enthusiast, so we're going to pretend to be from the Miniature British Rail Magazine, wanting to interview him. That should make him trust us enough to let us in. But once inside, it will be up to you to hypnotise him, and then to make him think that he's a Nazi.'

'I've got all that,' said Malcolm, 'but may I ask exactly *why* you want him to think that he's a Nazi?'

'That's not important right now,' said Elizabeth. 'All that matters is that you can convince him to believe that he's German, his father was a member of the SS, he follows Alt-Right on Twitter, and that you can make him do the occasional Nazi salute. Can you do it?'

'As I said on the phone, it will depend how susceptible he is to hypnosis, but it should be possible. I'll need to give him a trigger word though, to get him to do the salute.'

'How about when he hears people applauding him?'

'Yes, that should work.'

'Right! C'mon then. Let's see if he's in.'

They broke free from their umbrella huddle and crunched their way over Mr Webber's wide gravel drive, past a red Volvo estate, and up the stone steps to the front door.

McDongle pressed the bell and they all looked around at each other as they waited.

A few moments later, the door was pulled open and

there stood a small grey haired man wearing a crisp white shirt and a dark brown jumper.

'Mr Harold Webber?' asked McDongle, giving him his brightest of white smiles.

'Yes?'

'My name's Douglas, and this is Elizabeth and Malcolm. We're from the Miniature British Rail Magazine.'

'Oh, really!' exclaimed Harold, with obvious delight.

'Sorry it's unannounced, but a colleague told us you lived here, and that you were a bit of a collector, and so we thought we'd just drop by on the off-chance that we could see your collection and, hopefully, run a feature about you in next month's issue?'

'Well, yes, of course! Please, come in! Come in!' and he stepped backwards, beckoning them to enter.

'That's very kind of you. Thank you,' said McDongle, as he squeezed his way through the door frame.

'My collection is just through here,' said Harold, as he led them down the hallway. 'I seem to have amassed quite a few trains over the years. I'm sure you know what it's like.'

'Indeed we do,' said McDongle, as they headed towards the back of the house.

'I even had to have the house extended a couple of years ago to fit it all in.'

From his kitchen, they could see a large conservatory stretching out beyond, the centre of which featured a truly impressive model railway line that looked just like a tiny piece of England from the glory days of steam, with hills and valleys, bridges and tunnels, and tiny sheep dotted around a complex network of tracks and trains.

'Wow!' said McDongle, with unusual sincerity.

'That really is very impressive,' added Malcolm.

Elizabeth thought it looked like a childish mess of pointless junk that was doing nothing more than cluttering up what could have been a lovely conservatory. However, despite that, she joined in with the comments of approval by saying, 'It's *very* good, isn't it?' with only the slightest hint of sarcasm.

'Let me turn it on,' said Malcolm, 'then you can see it in action,' and he reached down to flick a switch beside a wall plug before bouncing back up to take hold of a series of red knobs on the side of the table. And as he slowly turned each one around, the various model trains began their journeys, albeit rather short ones.

And as the trains started to go round and around in seemingly endless, and to Elizabeth's eye, pointless circles, she elbowed Magic Malcolm as a signal for him to get started.

Signalling his understanding, Malcolm cleared his throat, and said, 'Mr Webber, if you could just focus on the big blue train for me.'

Surprised that the man hadn't used the correct name for that particular locomotive, Harold asked, 'You mean the Great Western 3803?'

'Er, yes, that one,' replied Malcolm.

'OK,' said Harold. 'What about it?'

'If you could just watch it go around for me.'

'Yes, of course. Are you going to take a picture of me?' he asked, as he began watching it go around.

'In a minute,' replied Malcolm, 'but for now I'd just like you to watch it go around for a while.'

'OK, well, I'm doing that. What next?'

'Just keep watching it. That's it. Good. Now I think you'll find that you're feeling sleepy, aren't you, Mr Webber?' asked Malcolm.

'Well, no, but I am feeling a little dizzy, if that helps.'

'If you could just keep watching it for me, as it goes out, and around, and back, and around, and out, and around, and back, and around, and out, and around, and back, and around, and out, and around, and back, and around.'

By this time, everyone in the room was nodding off, but Harold's head in particular looked as if it was beginning to slump forward where he stood.

'Now, as I count down from ten, you'll begin to feel increasingly sleepy,' said Malcolm. 'Ten…nine…eight…' but then he remembered that Harold would need to sit down, or else he'd just fall over when he reached one, so he gave Elizabeth a prod, who jumped with a start, and whispered to her, *'Can you find him a chair?'*

'Oh, sorry, yes of course,' and she skulked back into the kitchen as Malcolm continued with his countdown, but taking it a little more slowly to give her time to find one.

'Seven…….six…….five…….' he continued, and glanced over his shoulder to see how she was getting on.

Thankfully, she'd already returned, carrying a low kitchen stool.

'Will this do?' she whispered.

'It should,' he said, before keeping up with the count by calling out, 'Four.'

Looking back at Elizabeth, he said, *'If you could place it under him, and as he goes down, just guide him onto it. Then just make sure he doesn't fall off.'*

Elizabeth gave him a thumbs-up, and tiptoed over to where their host was still standing to gently ease the stool into a position under him where she felt he'd naturally sit, when that time came.

Meanwhile, Malcolm continued with, 'Three……..two…….and…….one.'

As he said that, Harold's head fell forward onto his chest, and Elizabeth eased him gently down, so that he was sitting, perfectly balanced on the stool.

'You're now in a deep state of hypnosis,' said Malcolm, hopefully, and was relieved when Harold agreed with him by mumbling, 'Yes, I am in a deep state of hypnosis,' almost as if he'd turned into some sort of a robot.

'Good,' said Malcolm, and delighted with his own performance, asked, 'I don't suppose I can have a cup of tea, could I?'

'Yes, you can have a cup of tea,' mumbled Harold again in his new, robotic sounding voice. 'I shall get one now for you,' and made as if to get up.

'NO! Not you! Sorry,' said Malcolm. 'You are in a deep state of hypnosis and you must stay where you are.'

'Yes, I am in a deep state of hypnosis and I must stay where I am,' obeyed Harold.

'I'm sure that someone else can get me a cup of

tea,' continued Malcolm, looking over at Elizabeth, who'd begun looking out at Mr Webber's garden.

'Yes, someone else can get you a cup of tea,' agreed Harold, with his robotic sort of a voice.

Malcolm leaned over towards Elizabeth, and whispered, *'I'll be about twenty minutes. I don't suppose you could pop the kettle on?'*

'Oh, yes of course. Sorry! How do you like it?'

'Milk, two sugars, thank you.'

And as Elizabeth went back out into the kitchen again, Malcolm continued with his hypnotic treatment of Harold.

'Now, Harold, you were born in Munich, weren't you?'

'No. I was born in Norwich,'

'Er, no Harold. You *were* born in Munich, in Germany.'

'Yes. I was born in Munich, in Germany.'

'Good. And your parents were German.'

'No. My parents were from Norfolk.'

'Again, that's not correct, Harold. Your parents *are* German.'

'Yes, my parents are German.'

'OK. Now, your father used to be a member of the Nazi Party. He also served as an officer in the SS. Isn't that correct, Harold?'

'No. My father was a Socialist, and an active member of the Labour party.'

'I'm sorry to contradict you, Harold, but your father *was* a member of the Nazi Party, and he *was* an officer in the SS.'

'I really don't think he was,' mumbled Harold.

'I can assure you that he *was*, Harold.'

Harold didn't reply to that, so to help reinforce the idea, Malcolm thought he'd add, 'And I can prove it as well, Harold.'

There was a moment's pause, before Harold's humanoid voice came back with, 'Can you show me your proof, please?'

'Er, no, Harold. You do not need to see my proof.'

'I'm fairly sure that I do.'

'No, Harold, you don't! You just have to trust me when I say that your father *was* a member of the Nazi Party and *did* serve as an officer in the SS.'

Another pause followed, a longer one this time. But then Harold's whole body twitched quite dramatically, and he mumbled, 'Yes, my father was a member of the Nazi Party and worked as an officer within the SS.'

'Excellent, Harold, excellent! Now we're making progress.'

Meanwhile, Elizabeth had come back into the conservatory holding a mug of tea.

'Here you go,' she whispered, handing it over to Malcolm.

'Thanks,' he said. *'He's displaying a little resistance, but overall it does seem to be working. Hopefully, I'll only need another ten minutes or so.'*

'No problem,' and with that, Elizabeth made a deliberate effort to catch the attention of McDongle, who'd been enjoying watching Malcolm's performance, and motioned for him to come out into the kitchen with her.

Leaving Malcolm to continue with his work, McDongle followed her out.

Leading him over to the kitchen table, she showed him a lap top surrounded by a pile of documents.

'I found this,' she said, picking up a particular white A3 piece of paper. 'It's the speech he's going to give at the town hall tomorrow, and it's been approved!'

McDongle took the document from her, glanced at it and asked, 'How do you mean, it's been approved?'

'You see this signature down here. That means that it's been officially signed off by the Labour party. All local election speeches must be approved before being given.'

'Oh, OK,' but McDongle glanced back down at it and said, 'So what?'

'So, I can forge the signature, which means that we can re-write his speech, to help it to align itself more with our own agenda.'

'Ah, yes, I see. Great idea!'

'Go back and tell Malcolm that we'll need Harold to stay under for a little longer, and I'll get to work on this.'

And with that, McDongle gave her his own thumbs up, which was larger, and more orange than hers, and waddled his way back into the conservatory.

CHAPTER TWENTY SIX
A TIME FOR CHANGE

THE DAY AFTER, and with nothing much else going on, Eliot asked Abigail and Will to cover the first of the by-election speeches that was due to be given in Portsmouth's Town Hall, by the Conservative and Labour Party representatives, Mr Douglas McDongle and Mr Harrold Webber, respectively.

'Is there really nothing else for us to cover?' asked Will, who had no interest in politics.

'I guess not,' replied Abigail.

Since their disastrous date a couple of days earlier, they'd hardly exchanged more than three words together. This lack of communication had been made easier by the fact that they'd had no more stories to cover, and had subsequently spent their working days together sitting opposite each other, hiding behind their computer monitors and trying to avoid getting up at the same time to go to the toilet.

This was the first time they'd been out on their own since, and as a result Will's question almost felt like a bit of an ice breaker.

They were sitting in the fifth row of folding chairs that had been laid out especially for the event, with an empty chair between them that they'd used deliberately to pile their coats onto, as well as their various bags and iPhones.

As the hall began to fill up with people, and the two candidates they'd come to see stepped up onto the

165

stage to sit on the vacant wooden chairs that had been left out for them, Will said to Abigail, 'It's a bit like going to the theatre, isn't it?'

He'd never actually been to the theatre before, but could imagine that it must have been a similar experience.

'Isn't it,' agreed Abigail, but as neither could think of anything else to say, they just sat there and watched everyone around them settle down.

It wasn't long before an elderly man joined the two candidates up on the stage, and crept along to the lectern that had been placed over to the far right. As soon as he was standing safely behind it, he raised one of his frail looking arms above his head as a gesture to help settle the audience and let them know that it was time to start.

Abigail leaned over to Will, and whispered, *'You'd better film this. We may be able to use it later.'*

'Welcome everyone,' began the speaker, 'to these, the first speeches that officially mark the beginning of the Portsmouth and Gosport by-election process.'

He paused to let the last two people in the audience finish their conversation, before continuing.

'As I'm sure you all know, the by-election has been called due to our former MP, Mr Michael Brownfield, being forced to stand down due to um, personal, er, problems, but here we have, standing in his place, their new representative, a Mr Douglas McDongle.'

McDongle gave the audience a half wave and flashed them all his incandescent white smile, but as nobody had a clue who he was, not even those Conservative Party Members present, the room remained deathly silent apart from just a single person, Elizabeth sitting on the back row, who initially started to applaud, but stopped very quickly when she realised she was the only one doing so.

'And the man sitting beside him,' continued the speaker, 'and standing as the Labour representative, is Mr Harold Webber.'

At least a handful in the audience new Mr Webber, and they gave him a spattering of applause which he acknowledged in much the same way as McDongle had done, but without the brilliant white smile.

'First to speak will be the Conservative representative, so if you could all give a warm welcome to Mr Douglas McDongle!'

McDongle's invitation to take his place behind the podium was at least met by a round of applause, this time, but as nobody apart from Elizabeth had any idea who the huge fat bald-headed man was who had to heave himself out of his chair to lumber his way over to the lectern looking very much like a genetically advanced tangerine wearing a suit, the applause was short lived.

Taking his position behind the lectern, McDongle took out the speech that Elizabeth had written for him, cleared his throat, and started to address them.

'Ladies and gentlemen,' he began, 'I'd firstly like to thank my predecessor, Mr Michael Brownfield, for his tireless work over the last few years, and I'm sure that we all wish him, and his wife, a full and speedy recovery.'

There was a weak murmur of approval from all those in attendance.

'Now I know that a lot of you are unaware as to who I am,' which, he thought, was hardly surprising, as he hadn't existed in his current form until the beginning of that week, 'and I'll be the first to admit that I don't know a huge amount about politics. My background is more, er…business orientated. But I can assure you that should you elect me, I'll be doing everything in my power to bring about sustainable economic growth for Portsmouth and Gosport by making this region an attractive place for companies to move into.

'I'll also be looking to build on the fine work done by my predecessor to continue to make this a clean and safe environment for young families to live and work. A crime free area that boasts a fine selection of outstanding schools and the very best in both national and private hospitals.

'But I also pledge to introduce an investment program to help reduce traffic congestion by encouraging people to either walk to work, or cycle. And I'll be looking to make significant local investments in our inner-city's infrastructure to create more pedestrian-only shopping areas, along with safe, bus-free cycle lanes, the combination of which I hope will encourage us to leave our cars at home more often.

'I'd like to thank you all for coming today, and I hope that I can count on your vote.'

As another ripple of applause resonated out from the audience, McDongle collected his speech, bowed his head in a way that he felt suited someone seeking a position in public office, and made his way back to his chair.

'What did you think?' asked Abigail, glancing around at Will.

'About what?'

'About Mr McDongle?'

'Oh, he seemed OK, I suppose,' he replied, but in fairness he hadn't been listening.

'You know, it's weird,' Abigail continued, 'but I can't help but think I've seen him somewhere before.'

'You probably have,' replied Will. 'He looks like the type who's been in and out of the news a fair bit.'

'Yes, I suppose, but there's something very familiar about him that I can't quite put my finger on.'

The old man had returned to his place behind the lectern to introduce the next candidate, so she put the thought out of her mind to continue listening.

'Thank you, Mr Douglas McDongle, thank you.' said the speaker. 'And now I'd like to welcome on stage the Labour Party's representative, Mr Harold Webber.'

As the audience gave Mr Webber another half-hearted round of applause, Harold got up from the wooden chair he'd been sitting on, stood to attention, gave them all a single Nazi salute, and marched over to the lectern.

'That was odd,' said Abigail to Will. 'Did you see that?'

But Will had been too busy filming to have noticed anything in particular, and as nobody else seemed to have either, she just assumed she must have imagined it, and settled back to listen to what he had to say.

As the applause abated, the Labour candidate shook

the hand of the old man who'd introduced him, and took his turn to stand behind the lectern. Removing some folded pieces of white A4 paper from his inside suit jacket pocket, he laid them out in front of him, straightened himself up and took a moment to gaze around at those in attendance.

'I'd firstly like to personally thank you all for coming today,' he began, with a strong, confident voice. 'I know that Portsmouth and Gosport has historically been a Tory seat, and so all those of us who support Labour's principals and ideology must feel a bit like the down trodden minority.'

There was a ripple of laughter that he let subside.

'But I also know that it takes courage to stand up for what you believe in, *especially* when those beliefs are not always shared by your family, friends, neighbours and colleagues.'

Another pause followed, as he took a moment to catch the eye of each and every person in the audience.

'However, what I've come to say to you today is that we are living in a time of change, and two of the biggest facing us today are those of unemployment and immigration.

'Portsmouth, our home, used to be the very hub of the British Empire, when Britannia ruled the waves and brought with it a flood of trade and jobs for our local community.

'But the tide turned a very long time ago, and after decades of local Tory government, we're now being flooded by neither trade nor jobs, but instead a steady stream of unwanted Eastern Europeans who have been, and continue to be allowed to cross our borders, unchecked, unregulated and not even counted up properly. And because of that, they've come over here, stolen all our jobs and have tried to rob us of our very national identity!

'But now's our chance to turn the tide back in our favour. A referendum's been held, and the people of Portsmouth and Gosport, along with the entire United Kingdom, have voted to leave the European Union, and to protect our borders in the process.

'If you vote for me,' he continued, 'I promise to do everything in my power to make sure our Government follows through with its promise to leave the EU, and to stop this seemingly endless flow of Eastern Europeans from invading our shores and taking our jobs. But not only that! As your local Member of Parliament, I'll promise to build a database that will identify all those living in Portsmouth and Gosport who are Eastern European by birth, and who are living here illegally. I'll then make sure we have some badges made up that will identify them, whilst we work towards rounding them up and having them sent back to where they came from.

'I also pledge, here and now, to build a giant fence, made of sustainable wood grown from British trees, that will stretch all the way from Gunwharf Quays to as far as Hayling Island, to act as an impenetrable barrier to any Eastern Europeans who think they can just float their way over the Channel on rafts made from non-biodegradable plastic milk bottles.

'And finally, if you vote for me, I'll do all that I can to persuade the Government to pour concrete into that obscene monstrosity that our neighbours up in

Kent built: the Channel Tunnel!

'Thank you once again for coming, and I hope to see you all out on Election Day.'

Much to Abigail's surprise, the entire audience, Labour supporters *and* Conservatives, leapt to their feet to give the Labour candidate a standing ovation, to which the man on stage began to return a series of what really did look like Nazi salutes.

'Are you recording all of this?' asked Abigail.

'Pretty much,' replied Will, who'd been intermittently losing concentration throughout, and probably had more footage of the back of the man's head in front of him than of those up on the stage.

'Didn't that all sound a little...well, xenophobically right-wing to you?' she asked him. 'You know, rounding up all the Eastern Europeans, making them wear badges, that sort of thing?'

Will just shrugged. For him, one political speech sounded very much like another, and he was able to phase most of them out, but he did at least think that the chap's salute was a little dated.

'C'mon,' she said. 'Let's see if we can get a few words with that last speaker,' and she stood up like everyone else, and began pushing and shoving her way through the audience, with Will tagging along behind her as he always seemed forced to do.

Reaching the wooden steps at the corner of the stage where Mr Webber had just began to descend in order to meet his doting audience, giving them all his very singular salute as he did so, Abigail called out, 'Mr Webber! Mr Webber!' as she dug out her microphone from inside her handbag. When she finally managed to reach him, she called out, 'Mr Webber! Can you tell us what it is exactly that you have against Eastern Europeans?'

As the applause was replaced by excited chatter, which at least enabled Harold to give his right arm a rest, he turned to look at Abigail, just as Will began filming behind her.

'Ah,' he said, 'Portsmouth's Youth! I hope you'll be voting for me in the forthcoming by-election?'

Ignoring his question, Abigail asked again, 'Can you tell us why you don't like Eastern Europeans, Mr Webber?'

'I have nothing against Eastern Europeans personally, it's just that they're a bunch of thieving miscreant bastards who should all be rounded up and shot.'

'I-I'm sorry, did you say "shot", Mr Webber?' asked Abigail, surprised by his choice of words.

'Well, no, of course not shot, exactly, but they do need to be executed by some means, there's no question about that!' continued Harold. 'Although, ideally I'd like to have them tortured first, of course.'

'I see,' said Abigail. 'But don't you think that's being a little extreme?'

'Not at all. In the last war, my father was an officer in the SS, and he'd round people up and shoot them all the time.'

'Really?' asked Abigail.

'Yes, well, admittedly they weren't Eastern Europeans,' continued Mr Webber, 'but I'm not sure that Europe had an eastern bit back then. But no doubt if it had, then he'd have treated them just like every other sub-human who wasn't a part of the Aryan Master Race.'

As Harold gave her a warm smile, for a moment Abigail was completely lost for words, and was certainly stuck for another question, so she turned to look back at Will's camera and decided to sum up her story by saying, 'This is Abigail Love, reporting from Portsmouth's Town Hall at the start of what should be a most interesting by-election.'

CHAPTER TWENTY SEVEN
WHY DON'T YOU COME BACK
TO MY PLACE?

AFTER THE LABOUR Candidate, Harold Webber, had finished his speech and had made his way down to meet his new clan of adoring members of the voting public, Douglas McDongle had remained up on the stage, slumped in his uncomfortable wooden chair.

At that precise moment in time he was feeling a little sorry for himself. In fact, he felt just about as miserable as he'd ever done in his entire life, which was saying something, giving his background. It was as if all his politically motivated hard work had come to nothing, and he was feeling that he may as well not have bothered to have gone to all the trouble of forcing a by-election by having the former Conservative MP for Portsmouth and Gosport, Michael Brownfield, and his wife, taken advantage of and subsequently hospitalised with the aid of two virile young Eastern European men and some superglue. And the whole episode of hypnotising the Labour Candidate into thinking that he was a Nazi had completely backfired!

And as he contemplated why the gods hated him so much, and just what he was going to do now, Elizabeth, who'd been quietly watching events unfold from the back of the hall, made her way up on to the stage.

Taking the empty seat next to his, she sat down beside her client.

'That didn't exactly go as planned,' she said, with an empathetic tone.

'No kidding,' replied McDongle.

'I mean, who'd have thought Portsmouth was crying out for a right-wing fascist dictator?'

'Evidently not us!'

Sensing McDongle's despondency, she took hold of his hand that looked like a sun-ripened Californian orange that someone had accidently trodden on, and said, 'Never mind, Douglas. It was only the first round. It's not over yet!'

'How can you possibly say it's not over yet?' He was clearly upset by the whole thing. 'It couldn't be more over if I'd just been flattened by a bus.'

'The election is still three weeks away,' said Elizabeth, in an effort to jolly the man up, 'and believe you me, a day in politics is a very long time indeed.' And patting his hand as if it was a tiny dog, she said, 'C'mon. Let's head back to my place. I've got at least one bottle of red with your name on it, and once there we can re-evaluate the situation and discuss a new plan of attack.'

After she'd driven him back to her house in her silver Nissan Micra, which McDongle had had a real struggle to get in to, and during which time she'd chatted to him about the weather that hadn't improved much since the evening before, he was planted down onto one of the floral-patterned sofas in her sitting room and given a generous glass of red wine to help boost his morale.

'Right then,' she said, as she poured out a glass for herself and eased down into the chair she would always relax in, either to read a gripping psychological thriller, or to listen to Radio 4, 'I've had a few ideas on the way here, the first one being to have some leaflets printed up. And then we'll be able to start handing them out at Cascades Shopping Centre at the weekend. And next week we can start taking them around to people's houses, which will give us a chance to speak directly to your voting public.'

But McDongle still wasn't in the mood to discuss something as demeaning as handing out leaflets, let alone deliberately going out of his way to talk to members of the general public. Instead, he pulled out the iPhone that had come with his new identity package, and did a Google search for "assassin for hire".

'Then I thought we could organise some more speeches,' continued Elizabeth, 'but maybe just speaking on your own this time.'

McDongle had stopped listening, and was instead focused on his internet search initiative that had just pulled up a promising 243,456 results.

I'd better try and narrow that down a bit, he thought, and added the word "Portsmouth" into the Google search field.

Did you mean Portsmouth, New Hampshire? the search engine asked him.

No, he thought, and included United Kingdom after Portsmouth.

No results for "Assassin for Hire Portsmouth United Kingdom"

Shit, he thought, and tried *"Assassin for Hire Portsmouth England"* instead.

No results for "Assassin for Hire Portsmouth England".

Unimpressed, he looked away from the screen to catch up with what Elizabeth was going on about.

'…and once we've invited them back for tea, you'd have a chance to get to know them more. And then you'd be able to chat about what your plans are for the local community.'

McDongle gulped down the entire contents of his glass of wine, replaced it on the coffee table in front of him, and asked, 'Can't we just hack into his computer, plant some pictures of half-naked children doing gymnastics, or something, and call the police?'

Pushing herself up from her chair, she picked up the bottle of wine, refilled his glass and sat back down.

'As I've already told you, Douglas, we need him to be able to stand. If he gets locked up, the chances are that everyone will vote for UKIP instead.'

But McDongle wasn't convinced, and the wine was only helping him to come up with increasingly darker plans other than giving out leaflets and organising tea parties. As far as he was concerned, the path towards becoming a Member of Parliament would be a whole lot easier if he was simply able to assassinate *all* his opponents, and with that in mind looked down at his iPhone again where, by chance, he saw a Google ad for a company called, WeKillAnyone.com.

Now we're talking, he thought, and tapped on the link that took him straight through to their website, on which was a global area search field.

Using his thumbs he typed in "Portsmouth United Kingdom", and tapped on the search button.

We have three results for Portsmouth, United Kingdom.

Excellent, he thought, and scrolled down to continue reading.

Please use the slide bar beneath to select how much you'd be willing to pay for your hired assassin.

Underneath was a bar which started at £10 and went all the way up to £5m.

OK, £5m is definitely beyond my budget, he thought, and moved the slider down to £10 and tapped on the "Go" button.

Up popped a black cut-out shadow image of a man whose name was, apparently, Psycho Phil. And underneath his name was written £20 per hit.

Thinking that was a reasonable amount, McDongle began to read the descriptive blurb about him.

"Psycho Phil is the very latest assassin to join WeKillAnyone.com. He's seventeen, lives in Fareham in Hampshire, and his hobbies include burning ants with a magnifying glass, shooting squirrels with his airgun, and torturing his younger brother with an elastic band and a pair of tweezers. He's yet to actually kill anyone, but is very keen, and his enthusiasm certainly makes up for his current lack of experience."

He sounds good, thought McDongle, sarcastically, and as he reached for his refreshed glass, realised that Elizabeth was still going on about something, so he thought he'd better listen in again, just in case he'd missed anything important.

'…and if we then took them all out to play bingo,

or maybe for a karaoke evening…'

He clearly hadn't, and as he phased her out once more, took a sip from his refreshed glass, placed it back down on the coffee table, and returned to the website to see who was available further up the price scale.

At the £250,000 mark came Backdoor Burt, who sounded more like some sort of a gay porn star than a trained killer, but as his choices seemed to be limited, he thought he'd better read through his description anyway.

"Burt is up for almost any job, and is in his element working either close up with a knife, or remotely using an explosive device. He's willing to travel anywhere within the South of England, but is unable to do international work as he doesn't have a passport. He's also unwilling to work with pets, children or women, but will happily eliminate old people of either sex."

He sounds OK, I suppose, thought McDongle, and clicked on the Booking button.

Unfortunately, Burt is fully booked until Christmas, but is now taking orders for the New Year.

'Oh for fuck's sake!' said Harold, but out loud, which he'd not meant to.

'Are you alright?' asked Elizabeth.

'Oh, yes. I was just thinking about, er, something else,' and he picked up his wine glass again, stared over at her and said, 'Sorry, you were saying?'

'Well, I was just suggesting that we could also take some of your supporters out to the theatre? There's a new musical in town, which I hear is quite good, but…I've been talking too much. Maybe you have some ideas of your own?'

He did, obviously, but had given up with the website WeKillAnyone.com and had decided that he'd be better off doing the job himself. Having reached that conclusion, and wondering where he might be able to pick up a gun, answered, 'Not really, no, but do you think I'd be able to borrow your car in the morning? I fancy doing a bit of shopping for myself.'

'Why yes, of course you can. I won't be needing it tomorrow. And maybe you'd like to, er, stay the night?'

Momentarily thrown off his guard, McDongle said, 'Th-that's very kind of you,' and by way of eager acceptance said, 'Thank you.' He couldn't even remember the last time he'd had sex, and certainly couldn't recall if there'd ever been a time when a woman had so obviously hit on him.

CHAPTER TWENTY EIGHT
IN A ROUNDABOUT SORT OF A WAY

'WHEN ELIOT SAID that they were going to start a news programme called *Trafficwatch*, I must admit that I thought he was joking,' said Will, as he stood next to Abigail in the middle of the Marketway Roundabout, just outside Portsmouth's main shopping area. 'Or at least I'd hoped he was, especially when he said that we had to do it first.'

'It's not *that* bad,' said Abigail, trying to be positive, as she watched streams of cars going round them in seemingly unending circles. 'At least they gave us a flask of coffee.'

'I suppose,' said Will.

After a few minutes of gazing at the various trucks, vans, buses, cars, taxis and bicycles that continued to go around them like modern day Native American Indians encircling a couple of Wild West settlers who were counting their bullets behind an overturned waggon, Will, becoming increasingly bored, asked, 'I don't suppose I could have some?'

'Huh?'

'Some coffee?'

'Oh, sorry. Yes, of course,' and she unscrewed the top, poured some out into the lid, and passed it over to him.

Taking a sip, Will thought he may as well clarify with her exactly what they were supposed to be doing there.

'So, the idea is that we stand here all morning, in the vague hope that someone has an accident, right?'

'Correct! Apparently there's at least one here every day, and they normally take place during rush hour.'

'I see,' said Will. 'Let's just hope we don't have to wait too long then, eh?'

'Hopefully not,' she agreed, and then thinking about timescales, asked, 'How long will that GoPro be able to keep filming up there?' as she looked up at the action camera they'd been given, along with the coffee.

'It should be good for three hours, give or take,' answered Will.

He'd been able to secure it onto a lamppost on the other side of the road using some gaffer tape that they'd also been given, and as high up as he could reach so that it could film the action as it (hopefully) took place.

'But when it runs out, I suggest we take lunch,' he added.

'Definitely. And maybe we could pick up some camping chairs to sit on from YouGet, at the same time.'

'Good idea,' said Will. 'And possibly a barbeque set, some burgers, and some tomato ketchup.'

'And we'd need some baps as well,', added Abigail, 'but I don't think they sell food at YouGet.'

'Probably not, but Safebusy's is only down the road.'

'True,' she agreed, but her attention had been caught by a small silver car that she'd noticed had circled the roundabout at least twice.

'Isn't that..?' she started to say, as she tried to get a

clear view of the face of the driver who was hunched up behind its steering wheel, alternating his gaze between the road ahead and a large unfolded map. 'Yes, it's that politician, you know, the one from yesterday, driving that car.'

'Which car?' asked Will, hoping to narrow it down.

'The tiny silver one.' She pointed as it continued to drive around them.

'Oh, you mean the 5-door Nissan Micra?'

'Yes, that one. But isn't that him?'

'Well, he's fat with an orange head, so it must be.'

'You know, I still think he looks familiar.'

'You did see him yesterday, Abi, so I'm not really surprised.'

'You know what I mean, Will. I swear I've seen him somewhere before. What was his name again?'

But Will didn't have a clue. He could hardly remember what he'd had for breakfast, let alone the name of some boring politician from the previous day.

'It was McDoogle, or something like that. Duncan McDoogle?' she asked herself as they watched him drive rather erratically round and round.

After a few minutes, Abigail asked, 'What on earth is he doing?'

'It looks like he's trying to read a map at the same time as drive a car that's clearly far too small for him. With a bit of luck, he's about to have an accident,' and in hopeful expectation, Will pulled out his iPhone to begin filming.

And it wasn't long before Will's wish came true.

As the driver attempted to come off the roundabout to turn into Commercial Road, he managed to knock some poor old chap off his bicycle.

'Told you,' said Will, feeling rather pleased with himself.

'Look, he's pulled onto the kerb. Let's see if we can interview him.' Taking the flask's cup lid from Will, she shook the remaining contents onto the grass, screwed it back onto the thermos and swapped it with the microphone in her handbag. She strode over towards the edge of the roundabout with Will following dutifully behind. And after managing to cross without getting knocked down themselves, they made their way over to the car where the old man still lay, with one leg caught underneath the bike.

'Are you sure you can't remember that guy's name?' she called out behind her.

'Who, the one with the bald orange head? No, I can't. But if you just shout out, 'Hey, Mr Tangerine Man,' and ask him if he can play a song for you, I'm sure he'll know who you're referring to.'

'I'm serious, Will.'

'Honestly, no, I can't remember. But it's definitely him though.'

'OK, look, I'm going to find out what his name is first, and then I'll go straight into covering the story. Got it?'

'Understood,' he confirmed, just as they reached the scene of the accident.

Stepping over the old chap, and his bike, Abigail looked across at the bald orange head of the driver who was half way out of his car.

'Duncan McDoogle, isn't it?' she called out.

'It's *Douglas McDongle*, actually!' said the man who

seemed to be a little irritated, and quite possibly stuck.

Turning back to Will, Abigail said, 'I knew it was something like that. Right, are you ready?'

'Yes, all set.'

'Are you sure?' she asked.

'It's definitely on, yes!' replied Will.

It was really beginning to piss him off that she kept asking him if his iPhone was filming all the bloody time. After all, he'd only forgotten to turn it on that once.

Shaking her hair out and licking her teeth, Abigail fixed a smile at Will's iPhone, and holding up her mic, said, 'This is Abigail Love, reporting from the scene of a horrific accident where Mr Douglas McDongle, who's currently standing as the Conservative representative in the forthcoming by-election, has just knocked down this poor elderly cyclist.' She then crouched down beside the man as he was endeavouring to push the bike off his leg, and asked, 'Are you all right?'

'Oh, yes, I think so. But thank you for asking.'

Leaving him to it, she stood up and stepped over to the car from where she could still see the back of the driver's large orange head which seemed to be hovering above the car's roof, in the same position as it had been before.

'Mr McDongle. It's Abigail Love, from Hampshire Today. May I ask why you deliberately ran over a cyclist?'

'I can assure you, Miss Love, that I did *NOT* do it deliberately, and if you could offer me some assistance in getting out of this bloody car, I'll gladly explain that to you.'

'Fair enough,' she said, and headed around to the other side where it became obvious that he was, indeed, stuck, and had only managed to get half way out. From a quick assessment of the problem, it was clear that the door frame was far too small for him. But as he already had managed to free his arms and was flailing around, a little like a giant orange octopus endeavouring to swallow a submarine, she decided to use one of them to pull him out, and went to replace her microphone into her handbag. But as cavernous as her bag was, it wasn't going to fit in, not with the coffee flask as well, so she swapped that with her microphone. But she was still one hand short of having two to pull the man out with, so she said to him, 'Would you mind holding this for me?'

'All right,' said McDongle. 'Would you like me to hold your handbag as well?'

She couldn't tell if he was being serious or not, so she said, 'No, I can manage that, thank you.'

With two hands now free, she took hold of one of his, rooted her feet securely onto the road as dozens upon dozens of cars, vans, buses and taxis continued to nudge their way past them, drivers and passengers gawping as they did, and announced, 'I'm going to start pulling you out, Mr McDongle. Are you ready?'

'Well, I'm hardly hanging around waiting for pizza,' the man replied.

But just as she was about to begin heaving him out, the penny dropped. She remembered where she'd seen him before! It had been outside Portsmouth Prison, where she'd been interviewing him after the prisoners had taken over and were holding the guards hostage. He'd said that they were demanding pizzas in exchange for the hostages. That was it, and this was him! The very same man, but a different colour and without the half-beard thing he'd worn back then. But he wasn't called McDongle then. No! He'd been called Morose, aka Chief Inspector Morose of the Solent Police, the very man who'd been found guilty of multiple murders and the one who'd only just started a forty-two year back-to-back life sentence before killing the prison warden with his bare hands.

In the middle of the horrifying epiphany that she was holding the hand of a deranged mass-murdering psychopath, she stopped where she was and just stared at him.

'Are you going to help me out or not?' McDongle asked, giving her an ominous look of malicious intent.

'Oh, yes, sorry, of course,' she said, and began pulling hard on his arm until, after a few strenuous moments of physical heaving, McDongle was finally able to wiggle his enormous backside out through the car's doorframe.

He was out!

Flattening down his suit and straightening his tie, he stared down at Abigail. 'Thank you!' he said, although it didn't sound as if he'd meant it, and handed the thermos flask back to her.

Taking it from him, she continued to stare up at him, with her eyes wide and mouth half open. Having made what could have possibly been the discovery of a lifetime, for a journalist at least, momentarily she didn't know what to do, say or think.

'Are you all right? McDongle asked, narrowing his fat little eyes at her. 'You look like you've seen a ghost.'

Fright snapped her out of it. Now that she knew who he was, the man had suddenly become truly terrifying. However, it was much more dangerous than simple psychological horror. If she recognised him, then he must know who she was as well, and that they had met before, in a previous life, for him at least! But if she continued to stare at him as she was doing she knew, deep down, that her life expectancy was plummeting by the second.

Fortunately for her, her brain worked faster than most, and she had a pure genius of an idea as to how to extricate herself from what had become a truly life-threatening situation.

'Ah…..ah…..ah…..' she started, before sneezing, and doing so just about as loudly as she could. At least, she pretended to.

Her brilliant idea was that the build-up to delivering a massive sneeze was the only plausible explanation anyone could ever have for staring at someone with their eyes and mouth open for the length of time that she'd been doing, other than, of course, if that person had just recognised that the man they were staring at was a mass-murdering psychopath who'd faked his own death and was now posing as a Conservative Party Candidate for a forthcoming by-election.

'Bless you,' he said.

'Thanks,' and she wiped her nose with the sleeve of her jacket. 'Sorry, where was I?'

'You were asking me why I'd deliberately knocked

down a cyclist.'

'Oh yes, that's right. Silly me! But maybe we should see if he's all right first?' she asked, now rather keen *not* to have to continue to interview the man.

'After you,' he said.

She nodded, and stepped around him with due caution.

By the time they'd navigated around to the other side of the car, the old man had managed to pick up both himself and his bike, and was busy straightening his cycling helmet.

'I'm most dreadfully sorry about that,' apologised McDongle, 'but I simply didn't see you.'

'That's quite all right,' said the cyclist. 'No harm done, and it's hardly the first time, which is why I wear this hat,' and straddling his bike again, he tapped on his cycling helmet, gave them all a cheerful smile, and rode off as if nothing had happened.

'Well, there we are then,' said Abigail, looking around at Will. 'I think you can stop filming now Will, and we can let Mr Moro-McDongle here get back on the campaign trail,' and although she had very nearly let the proverbial cat out of the bag, and becoming ever more desperate to get as far away from the Incredible Orange Psycho-Hulk as possible, she forced herself to ask, 'How's it all going, anyway?'

'Very well, thank you for asking. I was actually just off to buy a, er, to see about printing up some leaflets.'

'Then I'll leave you to it. C'mon, Will, we'd better get back on traffic watch. Nice to meet you Mr McDongle,' she said, and focussed on the challenging task of re-crossing the road.

CHAPTER TWENTY NINE
DEMONSTRABLE PROOF

ONCE SAFELY BACK on the roundabout, Abigail watched McDongle out of the corner of her eye, as he squeezed himself back into his car and drove off to continue his journey down Commercial Road.

As soon as he was out of sight, she turned to Will and said, 'That was close.'

'No kidding!' agreed Will. 'If he'd killed that cyclist, then Mr Tangerine Man's political ambitions would have been over.'

'That's not exactly what I meant,' said Abigail. 'When I was helping him out of the car, I remembered where I'd seen him before.' With a grave, solemn look, she whispered to him, *'He's Morose!'*

'He's morose?' asked Will, with no real idea what she was going on about.

'That's right!'

'But…so what? I'd have thought that any politician would be bad-tempered and a bit gloomy if they'd just been caught on-camera, stuck half-way out of their miniature car after knocking some old man off his bike.'

'No, not *that* sort of morose. *The* Morose!'

'The Morose, who?'

'The old Chief Inspector Morose, the one found guilty of multiple murder.'

'B-but…he's dead, isn't he?' asked Will. 'I mean, we

found his body, down on the beach, and he'd definitely passed away because his head was missing.'

'Yes, I know, but I swear to you; that *was* Morose!'

'But Abi, we only found him on Monday, and generally speaking, people's heads just don't grow back that quickly.'

Ignoring his badly timed attempt at humour, Abigail went on, 'Somehow he must have faked his own death, but I can assure you that Douglas McDongle is *definitely* Morose!'

'And you're sure, Abi, I mean, *really* sure?'

'I'm absolutely one hundred percent positive!'

'Bloody hell!'

There was a pause in their conversation as Abigail gave Will time to digest that extraordinary piece of information, and after a few moments of gazing out at the traffic, he said, 'It's certainly one hell of a story.'

'I know.'

'But only if you can prove it,' he added, as he turned back to face her.

It was Abigail's turn to stare out at the endlessly circling commuters, as her brain's synaptic nerve endings exploded into life in a desperate bid to fathom a way that she could.

'Any chance of another coffee?' asked Will, who'd already managed to by-pass the problem, and was instead thinking that he could do with another drink.

'Huh?' asked Abigail, lost in thought.

'Coffee, from the flask?' asked Will again, and pointed at the thermos that was still in her hand.

Abigail stared down at it.

'My God!' she exclaimed. 'Of course! Will, you're a

bloody genius!'

'Er, yes, I know, but I'm not sure how asking for some coffee is the best way to determine my IQ.'

'McDongle, I-I mean Morose, held the flask!' Abigail exclaimed. 'I gave it to him, and he held it. So it's going to have his fingerprints all over it!'

The thermos flask she was holding in her now trembling hand had the potential to prove, beyond all reasonable doubt, that Douglas McDongle, the Conservative Party's representative for Portsmouth and Gosport's forthcoming by-election, was none other than the Psychotic Serial Slasher of Southampton and the South Coast, a man who until that precise moment in time had been presumed dead by the entire British community and beyond.

With the utmost care, and so as to not contaminate the evidence any more than she must have already done, she rested the base of the flask on her free hand and peeled the other from its side so that she could use one of its fingers to balance it from the top. Having done that, she said, 'Will, get the GoPro. We're taking this down to the police station to ask them to check it for fingerprints.'

'But what about *Trafficwatch*?' he asked. After all, it was common knowledge to never go anywhere near a police station unless it was absolutely necessary, or unless, of course, you'd just been nicked.

'Sod bloody *Trafficwatch*,' said Abigail. 'What I have here, in my very hands, is quite possibly the biggest story of our lives. And besides, Eliot only asked us to cover one accident, and thanks to Mr Douglas McDongle, we've already done that.'

CHAPTER THIRTY
CLEAR LINE OF SIGHT

AFTER SPENDING a good two hours driving around Portsmouth, looking for somewhere that sold hunting rifles, during which time he'd circled numerous roundabouts, too many of them more than once, and on one of which he'd managed to knock some poor old man off his bike, and had been caught by Hampshire Today doing so; after all that, he'd finally been able to find a suitable retailer. It was called Harry Kari's Fishing & Hunting Centre, just off of Spring Street.

As it turned out, they not only sold guns, but also had a fine selection of fishing equipment which included rods, reels and bait, as well as camouflaged waterproof clothing, a variety of khaki green collapsible camping chairs, and waterproof plastic explosives for fishermen who were in a bit of a hurry.

They also had a truly excellent sales team, and he'd emerged from the retailer with not only the gun he'd gone in for, a Rodney .275 Stalking Rifle with a detachable silencer and two boxes of cartridges, but also an Arc Angel fishing rod, a decent sized landing net and some bait. He'd always fancied taking up fishing, and he was now fully equipped to do so, just as soon as he'd made the successful transition into becoming an elected Member of Parliament.

With that goal now firmly in his mind, he made his way back to the car to seek out the man he felt was standing in his way, Mr Harrold Webber. But when buying all the new gear, he'd forgotten about his current mode of transport, and just how small it was. After all, there was barely enough room for him on his own, let alone a rifle, the fishing rod and the landing net, none of which seemed to be collapsible, and if they were, he couldn't work out how.

So with life's various hunting essentials sticking out of half-opened car windows he set off back to 6, Hellene Road to locate his prey and wait for an appropriate opportunity to shoot him, preferably straight through the head.

Arriving outside Mr Webber's house, close enough to be able to view his front door without being observed doing so, he was just in time to see Harold make his way out, carrying a large cardboard box which he placed into the boot of his red Volvo Estate before driving away.

Without making it obvious what he was up to by using specialist surveillance techniques taught to him during his time with the police, McDongle followed behind in his heavily accessorised silver Nissan Micra, hoping that at some point his quarry would park up somewhere suitable for him to get a clear shot, and without too many people seeing him do so.

It wasn't long before he had his opportunity, because as it turned out, Harold Webber was out doing some good old fashioned door-to-door canvassing, and his first stop was a quiet cul-de-sac called Turnpike Crescent, just off Stubbington Avenue.

McDongle crept to a halt before the turning into the road. He didn't want to commit himself by driving into such a small residential area that only had one exit, at least not until he knew what Harold was doing there; but as soon as he saw him step out of the car, grab a handful of Labour leaflets from the cardboard box in the boot, along with a clipboard, and stride off towards the first of the small semi-detached houses, he knew his opportunity had come. So he slowly drove the car in, and all the way around, before parking it so that it was facing out. He did this for two reasons. Firstly it would mean that he could drive straight out after the job had been done, without risking the need to do a three-point turn, and secondly, because he'd be able to aim the rifle at the eight houses on the car's passenger side, but without having to poke the whole gun out of the window to do so.

Leaving the engine on but taking his seat belt off, and after a fair bit of faffing about with loading the gun's magazine and screwing the silencer onto the end of its barrel, he was all set. But by that time Harold was already at the door of 3, Turnpike Crescent, and there were only five houses left before he'd need to re-park on the other side, and no doubt attract unwanted attention to himself as he did.

Without further ado, McDongle electronically wound down the front passenger window, and did the very best he could to swivel himself around in the driver's seat so that he could secure the butt of the rifle firmly against his shoulder. He relaxed his neck before resting his fat orange cheek against the gun's stock, and using one eye, glared down the length of the barrel, so that the bead at the end was lined up with the crook that was about half way along. Having managed to position himself correctly, he homed in on his target.

Harold, meanwhile, was busy chatting to the elderly man at the door, who seemed to be either very keen to find out more about Harold's electoral pledges, or was a bit deaf and was struggling to hear anything at all. From where McDongle was positioned, it was difficult to tell. But now was his chance, and with his heart pounding hard in his chest, he did his best to control his breathing, rested his finger on the trigger and squeezed.

'Fuck it,' he thought.

At the very last minute, Harold turned away to head back down the path, and McDongle managed to shoot the old man instead, straight through the head. Fortunately, for McDongle at least, the force of the bullet pushed the man backwards, so that he disappeared inside the house, somehow managing to close the door as he did so.

As quietly and as quickly as he could, McDongle lifted the rifle's bolt, and eased it back so that another cartridge could be pushed into the firing chamber by the magazine underneath. He then eased the bolt forward and brought it down to lock it into place, and lifted the butt to bring it back against his shoulder to re-discover his target.

By the time he'd done all that, Harold had already made his way around to the next house and was halfway up the garden path approaching its door.

This time McDongle wasn't going to wait a second longer than he had to, and as soon as Harold stopped, and his head was lined up in his sights, he pulled the trigger.

However, he was unaware that before he was able to do that, the door opened; the man inside, a heavy-set middle aged chap, saw that it was just some stupid Labour candidate, and slammed it shut again. Judging by the way that Harold's head shifted back, the householder must have told him to fuck off, or something. Whatever he'd said, the result was the same. McDongle missed his target once more, but had a very strong suspicion that he'd managed to shoot yet another innocent person, and again straight through the head.

'For fuck's sake,' he muttered. Fuming with anger at himself and life in general, he reloaded a third cartridge into the firing chamber and prepared for another shot. To do this he needed to change from aiming out of the front passenger side window to the one at the back, and once that was fully wound down it was clear that not only was Harold further away, but the angle wasn't nearly as good as it was before. McDongle also had the steering wheel to contend with, as well as the passenger seat's headrest, his fishing rod and his landing net, both of which were sticking out of the same back window.

He was also struggling to maintain the sort of steady composure needed to be a good marksman, probably because he was losing both his patience and temper. Subsequently, his next shot was wide by a long way, and shattered the frosted glass that ran vertically down the side of the next house's front door, and it did so just as Harold began chatting with the lady inside.

At the door of the house, it looked as if neither Harold nor the lady suspected that the thing that broke the glass was a bullet; after all there had been no sound of a shot fired thanks to McDongle's silencer. They were both staring at the hole in the window, probably trying to work out what had made it implode like that.

McDongle took the opportunity to reload once again, and having done so, took aim and fired. This time he hit a drainpipe, which must have been made of metal, as the bullet ricocheted off and buried itself into the arm the lady had been using to hold the door open. McDongle could tell, because she clutched at it with the hand that was attached to her other arm. And when she pulled it away and saw that it was covered in blood, she gazed wide-eyed at Harold standing directly in front of her and let out a blood curdling scream.

'Fuck, fuck, fuck, fuck, fuck, fuck, fuck,' said McDongle to himself, and reloaded just as fast as he possibly could to take aim at Harold's head, which seemed to have become transfixed by the blood dripping from the lady's elbow, and pulled the trigger. He missed again, so much so that he didn't even see where the bullet ended up. With renewed screaming from the woman, and Harold still standing up, and not keeling over to start pushing up daisies in the lady's front garden, McDongle thought he'd better make the best of a bad day and get the hell out of there. After ditching the gun in the back seat, as best he could, he put his seat belt back on, jammed the gear lever into first and drove off.

Meanwhile, at the front door of 5, Turnpike Crescent,

as the lady continued screaming at him for no particular reason, other than that she'd somehow managed to hurt her arm, her right ear had started to bleed and a wall mirror inside her hall had just exploded, Harold thought he'd better take her inside, patch her up, and try to calm her down a little. She was clearly worked up about something, and it couldn't have been just because he was the Labour candidate for the forthcoming by-election. If it had only been that, she'd have simply slammed the door on his face like most people did, not attack herself in a bout of self-harm, accompanied by a series of screams with wailing and sobbing thrown in for good measure.

So, he took her through to her kitchen, where he ran her arm under a cold tap. And although this didn't stop her from staring at him as if he was Dr Hannibal Lecter who'd just popped by for something to eat, it did at least calm her down enough for him to put her kettle on, give her one of his leaflets and start to tell her about his electoral pledges for the local area.

CHAPTER THIRTY ONE
CAN I HAVE YOUR AUTOGRAPH?

WITH WILL OPENING the heavy glass door for her, Abigail made her way into the lobby of Solent's police station, carrying the flask of coffee between her two hands as she'd been doing before, as if it was a nuclear warhead she'd just found out in the car park.

Sitting behind the reception desk, directly in front of her, was Solent Police's Duty Sergeant, who was staring at a large flat screen TV that was secured to the wall on their right, above a currently empty row of blue plastic seats.

As she walked through the door, he turned to look at her and did a bit of a double take, exchanging looks from the TV and back. He then pointed straight at her and said, 'Blimey! You're Abigail Love, ain't ya?'

Not used to being recognised out on the street, or in this instance, inside the lobby of her local police station, Abigail went a little pink around the edges and said, 'Yes, er, I am, I suppose,' and made her way over to the desk, with Will following behind.

The duty sergeant continued, 'I've just been watching you on TV.'

'Have you?' she asked, with a level of nonchalance she felt to be expected from a local celebrity, and rested the coffee flask on top of the desk.

'You're on now. Look!' he said, pointing at it with the remote control.

Abigail and Will both turned to watch, as their coverage of the first by-election speeches was being shown.

'I don't suppose I can have your autograph?' he asked, as he pushed a notepad towards her, along with a blue and white Solent Police pen.

'Really?' she said, glancing up at Will, almost as if to ask for his permission.

Will tried hard to look like he really didn't give a shit what she did.

'If you wouldn't mind, Miss Love?' the duty officer asked, and in a manner that suggested that if she didn't, he'd have her arrested for being intentionally obstinate, or something.

With a shrug, Abigail picked up the pen, thought for a moment, and then wrote something down before turning it around and pushing it over to him for his approval.

'Thanks!' he exclaimed, as he read what she'd written.

"To the policeman behind the reception desk at the Solent police station, Warmest regards, Abigail Love."

When he'd finished reading it, he turned it around and pushed it back towards her, saying, 'My name's actually Ian.'

Apologising, Abigail crossed out, "the policeman", and above wrote "Ian", before turning it around once more for him to see.

After reading it again, he gave her a toothy grin. 'Is it alright if I take a photo of you as well, Miss Love?' he asked, and began searching his pockets for his smartphone.

'I don't think…um,' she started, looking up at Will again, who rolled his eyes at her before using them to direct her towards the coffee flask, as a reminder as to why they were there.

This prompted her to say, 'We'd actually come to ask for your assistance with something.'

'It won't take a sec,' continued the duty sergeant, and with his smartphone found, made his way around the high desk.

Standing next to her as he held the camera phone at arm's length, he brought his head down so that it was level with hers, and when he saw that they were both in the frame, took the picture.

'That's great!' he said, checking that the photo looked OK, before returning to the other side of the desk.

Before the policeman had a chance to ask for anything else, like a pair of her pants, or a signed photocopy of her naked bum, Abigail thought she'd better push on.

'I don't suppose it would be possible for you, er, Ian, to run a fingerprint check on this thermos flask?' she asked, looking at the object in question.

'Hold on,' he said, still staring at his camera. 'I'm just sharing it onto Facebook.'

As he did that, Abigail gazed up at the TV to see that they were now showing her interview with the Labour candidate, Harold Webber.

A moment or two later, the duty sergeant said, 'Right, that's done. I'll just post it up to Twitter, Google plus, Pinterest, Tumblr, Flickr and Reddit, and then I'll be with you.'

For fuck's sake, thought Abigail. 'You do know that you can do all that on Instagram, don't you?' she asked him.

'Really?'

'Yes, of course!' she said.

'How do you do that?'

'Have you got an Instagram account?'

'I do, yes, but I haven't had a chance to use it yet.'

'Well, look, it's all very straightforward. Instead of uploading a photo to each different site, you can just share it onto Instagram and it will automatically send it out to all your social media accounts.'

'Honestly?'

'That's right. And you can even customise the image before you send it!'

'Blimey!' he said, with genuine astonishment. Although he found it difficult to keep up with the perpetual onslaught of 21st Century technological advancement, he did at least think it was all fascinating, none the less.

'Yes, of course!' said Abigail, looking at the man as if he was a hashtag short of a Twitter update.

'Er,' interrupted Will. 'I don't suppose we could possibly move on to what we came here to talk about?' he asked. It wasn't that he was particularly keen to move forward with their journalistic investigation, but he'd no interest in social media, and was hoping that they could get the thermos flask checked over, so that he could finally get that coffee he'd been waiting for ever since Abigail had discovered the significance of the flask.

Realising she'd allowed herself to be distracted,

Abigail said to the policeman, 'Tell you what, if I show you how to use Instagram, is there any chance you could have someone run a fingerprint check on this thermos flask?'

The duty sergeant stared at her, and then at the flask.

'Well, it's against police policy to undertake forensic investigative work on behalf of the press,' he said, with a tone of formality that, until then, had been somewhat lacking.

'Yes, I'm sure, but if you do, I'll show you how you can personalise every picture you take on Instagram *before* you send it out!'

'You'd be able to do that?' he asked.

'If you run a fingerprint check for me, then yes, I would.'

The duty sergeant looked down at his smartphone, up at the thermos flask, down at the phone again and then up at Abigail. 'OK. Just this once.' And as he reached under the desk to retrieve a large clear plastic evidence bag to place the flask into, asked, 'Are the fingerprints of anyone in particular that you're looking for?'

'Damn right they are,' she said, with a determined look, and grabbed the remote control before using it to point up at the wall-mounted TV. Pausing the Hampshire Today news broadcast that was currently showing their lead anchor, Marcus Thornbury, reading from the teleprompter as he was paid to, she re-wound it all the way back to the footage that had been playing when they'd walked in, which was of McDongle's speech, before the part when Abigail had interviewed

Harold Webber.

'I believe,' she continued, 'that *that man there* is none other than Morose, the former Chief Inspector of the Solent Police, otherwise known as the Psychotic Serial Slasher of Southampton and the South Coast!'

'What, *him?*' asked the duty sergeant, pointing up at the paused image of the giant-sized bald-headed orange man in the immaculate dark blue suit.

'That's right, *him!*'

'I'm sorry, Miss Love, but you're mistaken. I'd recognise Morose anywhere, and apart from the fact that his headless body was found on the beach, he had white skin, not orange. He also had normal coloured teeth. And the last time I saw him, he had a half-beard thing as well.'

But Abigail wasn't in the mood for an argument. She knew it was the same man, and the fingerprints on the flask would prove it; and knowing that, she said, 'I'm sure you're right, Ian, but could you perhaps humour me?'

'So, you want me to run a print check off of that flask, to see if we can get a match with the deceased Chief Inspector Morose?' he asked, for clarification.

'If you could, yes please,' and she gave him one of her most vivacious smiles.

'And in exchange, you'll show me how to use Instagram?'

'I will.'

There was a moment's pause, as they both stared at each other.

'OK. You've got a deal,' he said, and picked up the receiver of the phone on his desk, dialled what must have been an extension number, and said, 'Can you send someone up to reception, please? We have some evidence that needs a full fingerprint analysis. Thank you.'

He replaced the receiver, but only to hear it ring again. So he picked it up, and said, 'Solent Police?'

After about five seconds, he asked, 'Where are you calling from?'

As he listened, he tore off the top sheet of his notepad, the one with Abigail's signature on it, and started taking frantic notes.

'And is that the same location as the shooting?' he asked the caller. 'OK, I'm going to put you on hold for just one moment, but don't go away.' With that, he pressed a series of buttons on the telephone's keypad, paused, and then said, 'Chief Inspector Chupples, it's Jackson here, Sir. I'm afraid there's been a report of a shooting.'

CHAPTER THIRTY TWO
POLICEBOT

IT WAS ALL hands on deck at the Solent Police station. Rarely had there been a reported shooting in Portsmouth, not for many years, and after making sure that the thermos flask had been bagged, tagged and picked up by forensics, Abigail rushed out to their van, with Will doing his very best to show a similar level of motivation by walking after her a little faster than normal.

Following the various police cars to the scene of the reported incident, they arrived just outside Turnpike Crescent, off Stubbington Avenue, where they parked up on the kerb, as had all the other police cars along with three ambulances, a fire truck and two AA vans. But nobody from any of the emergency services seemed to be keen to actually enter the cul-de-sac, either on foot or otherwise, not until they'd had a chance to find out a little more information about who the reported shooter was, and if the criminal had a real gun, or just some sort of an air rifle.

Seeing a group of policemen, some wearing uniforms and others in plain-clothes, gather around another, with an expectation that they were about to be briefed, Abigail and Will wandered over towards them, just close enough to overhear what, if anything, was about to be said.

'Listen up, men,' said a fastidious-looking policeman wearing an elaborately decorated uniform and a peaked cap. 'This is the entrance to Turnpike Crescent, where the reported shooting is said to have taken place. Now, the person who called in said that the gunman took a hostage into Number 5. We've had a look on Google Maps and it's a cul-de-sac, so the only exit is this one, unless he escapes through the garden. However, we've already taken the precaution of sending another armed unit around to Stubbington Golf Course, situated behind, to ensure that that particular escape route is blocked.

'We don't know much more than that he has some sort of a weapon, and has taken at least one person hostage inside the house. I'm not prepared to take any chances with any of your lives, or the lives of any hostages inside, so I propose that we send Policebot in first, to do some initial reconnaissance, prior to us going in.'

There was a general murmur of approval from all those in attendance, apart from Abigail and Will, who were pretending not to be listening.

'OK,' continued the person in charge, 'who here holds a Policebot controller license?'

Two hands went straight up, one wearing a uniform and the other plain-clothed who Abigail recognised from the unfortunate incident involving the former MP, Michael Brownfield.

'Right. Constable Sparrow, you take control of the Policebot, and Sergeant Dewbush, you can keep an eye on the monitor.'

'But Sir!' protested the one he'd called Dewbush. 'I'm much better at controlling it than Sparrow is, Sir! I've even got my own remote controlled battlebot at home, Sir, and I'm always watching Robot Wars. Please, Sir, can't I control it?'

'I don't know, Dewbush.'

'*And* my rank is higher than Sparrow's, Sir!'

'Very well. But we're just using it for reconnaissance, Dewbush. Do you understand?'

'Yes, Sir. I understand, Sir. Thank you, Sir,' said the policeman called Dewbush, and Abigail saw him give the one called Sparrow a belittling smile that must have indicated some sort of personal victory.

Leading Will away from them in order to have a quite word, Abigail said, 'I suggest we wait until they get that robot out, and then we can sneak in whilst they're all distracted by it. That way we might be able to land an exclusive interview.'

'An interview with who?'

'With the gunman, of course!'

'Are you completely mad?' asked Will, becoming convinced that she must be. 'They've just said that he's armed and has at least one hostage. You're not seriously suggesting that we go in there, find him and then ask if he wouldn't mind having a chat with us, are you?'

'Well, I don't see why not. They've already told us what house he's in, and besides, all these deranged psycho nut-jobs want to be famous, so I'm sure he'd agree.'

'B-but…' stuttered Will, desperate to persuade her otherwise, 'what if he just takes us hostage as well?'

'But he won't. He'd never be able to get his story out if he did.'

'Yes, but what if he's not interested in being

famous, and just wants to kill as many people as possible before being locked up? Have you thought of that?'

'Honestly, Will. I've done this a hundred times before.'

She'd never actually done it even once, prior to what she was now proposing, but she didn't think that that was relevant; and besides, she'd read enough psychological thrillers to know that all psychopaths ever wanted was to be famous, and concluded her argument by saying, 'If they didn't want all the fame, then they simply wouldn't bother!'

Having decided that she'd won the debate, she glanced over her shoulder to see a large blue and white rectangular shaped remote-controlled vehicle with POLICEBOT written down its side and a GoPro camera stuck on its roof, begin to rumble slowly down Stubbington Avenue towards the entrance to Turnpike Crescent.

'C'mon,' she said, 'we can skirt around the side here, and I reckon we'd have reached Number 5 before it's even turned the corner.' So saying, she stepped casually over a low brick wall and began wading her way through the undergrowth on the other side.

Will let out a heavy sigh. He'd no intention of being considered a wimp by his nemesis from school, even though he was trying hard not to care what she thought about him, and so he felt he had little choice but to follow.

She was right. It took them no time at all to creep over to the first house and then across four front gardens to reach the door of the fifth. But as Abigail raised her hand for the doorbell, Will stopped her.

'Are you absolutely sure you know what you're doing, Abigail?'

'Trust me,' she said, and gave him one of her beguiling smiles that would have hypnotised any man into doing whatever she'd proposed, no matter how stupid or potentially life-threatening. She was just about to press the buzzer, when they heard the Policebot trundle its way around the corner and into the peaceful cul-de-sac, heading straight at the house in front of which they were now standing.

Unsure as to whether or not it would be able to see them, they separated to hide behind adjacent garden shrubs that lined the path to the house. Peeking around, they saw the Policebot stop in the middle of the virtually empty road, before it started to do a full 360 degree turn.

Then they heard another similar whining noise, coming from one of the houses on the other side, and which was accompanied by what sounded like some sort of a two-stroke engine.

'Did they say they had two Policebots?' whispered Will to Abigail, as they continued to hide behind their respective bushes.

'I only heard them say they had one,' whispered Abigail back.

'Well, I can hear something that sounds a bit like another.'

Just then the Policebot stopped going around in a big circle. It, too, must have seen something, as it was pointing directly at Number 11, on the other side of the circular road.

Will raised his head above the shrub in an attempt to see what it was looking at.

'It's another robot!'

'Another Police robot?' asked Abigail, who was doing the same, but her view was blocked by a red Volvo estate.

'No,' said Will. *'It looks like one of those battlebots from off the telly.'*

'Really?'

'I think so.'

Although not a huge fan, Will had watched a number of episodes of Robot Wars, as had most men, and could certainly recognise a battlebot when he saw one.

'It's got the name Private Parts written down its side,' he whispered, adding, *'and what looks like a chainsaw on its roof.'*

Will was right, and it wasn't long before Abigail could also see a skin-coloured battlebot in the shape of a human male's scrotal sack, with what did indeed look like a chainsaw mounted on its roof spluttering blue smoke out from its exhaust, as it rumbled its way ever-closer to the Policebot that seemed to be just waiting for it.

'I think they're going to fight!' said Will, who was clearly becoming excited by the prospect of watching a real-life episode of Robot Wars.

'Don't be so stupid,' said Abigail, and lifted her head above the bush so she could see both robots. She was just in time to see the skin-coloured one raise up its chainsaw as it buzzed and screamed into life to begin a full frontal attack of what it must have considered to be an enemy robot that had crossed some kind of territorial boarder.

'Boys!' bemoaned Abigail, and stood up to reach for the doorbell again.

'Don't!' called Will, but he was too late, and they both heard the gentle muffled sound of a *"ding-dong"* echo from inside the house.

As the battle began between Policebot and Private Parts in the middle of Turnpike Crescent, the door of Number 5 was opened, and Will stood up to join Abigail as they were greeted by a peculiar-looking woman in a light blue nightie, with a plaster over one ear and what looked to be a blood-soaked piece of kitchen paper held against her right arm. In her free hand she clutched a Labour leaflet, and the fact that she had a distant, almost vacant expression, combined with the leaflet and outfit choice, made her look as if she'd just joined the Labour Party having recently escaped from a high-security insane asylum.

'H-hello?' she asked, as she stared first at Abigail, and then at Will.

'Sorry to disturb you,' said Abigail, 'but we were wondering if we could talk to the man who's taken you hostage?'

'Oh, yes, of course,' she said. 'I'll just go and get him for you.'

As soon as she'd turned away, Abigail began rummaging around in her handbag for her microphone.

Will, meanwhile, had become distracted by the battle raging behind them, and was trying to see who'd gained the upper hand. So Abigail gave him a nudge with her elbow, and whispered, *'Will, your camera!'*

As it was fairly obvious that although Policebot was putting up a good fight, Private Parts was bashing the mechanical shit out of it, he pulled out his iPhone, turned it on, and took a step back so that he could fit both Abigail and the still open door into the shot.

Moments later, Harold Webber came ambling up the narrow hallway towards them, saying, 'You wanted to see me?'

Somewhat taken aback that the gunman was non-other than the xenophobic right-wing Labour candidate for the Portsmouth and Gosport constituency, Abigail spun around to stare at Will's camera phone.

'This is Abigail Love, reporting from 5, Turnpike Crescent, in Portsmouth.'

'How did you know I was here?' asked Harold, completely taken by surprise by the sudden and wholly unexpected appearance of the media.

Ignoring his question, Abigail continued talking to Will's iPhone.

'We're delighted to have with us today Mr Harold Webber, who's currently running for Labour in the forth-coming by-election.'

She then turned to face Harold, who still looked to be in complete shock.

'Mr Webber, it's been reported that you've shot a number of people in the local area, and that you've now taken some poor woman as a hostage. Is that true?'

'W-what?' he asked, looking even more surprised than he'd done before.

'Is it true that you've been on a massive killing spree, and you've now gone to ground inside what looks to be a two bedroom detached house in Turnpike Crescent?'

'What on earth are you going on about?'

'So, you're not going to deny it then?'

'No, I-I mean yes! Of course I'm going to deny it!'

'Then how can you explain the reports that you're none other than Hatchet Harry, the Cul-de-sac Killer of Turnpike Crescent?'

Having made that up on the spot, Abigail had surprised herself by just how good a title it was.

'Have you completely lost your mind?' he asked, but behind her something had caught his eye, and it wasn't a scrotum-shaped battlebot doing a victory spin out in the middle of the road.

Along both sides of the crescent he could see what looked remarkably like armed police, sneaking their way between shrubs, bushes and cars as they made their way into the cul-de-sac towards the house he was standing in.

Just then, over some sort of tannoy system, came a tinny voice. *To the gunman inside Number 5, Turnpike Crescent. This is an armed unit of the Solent Police. We have you surrounded. Please step away from the hostages with your hands in the air.*

'Any last words, Mr Webber?' asked Abigail, raising her microphone for him to speak.

Turning visibly pale, and as he slowly lifted his now trembling hands above his head, he spluttered out, 'B-b-but this must b-be some sort of a t-terrible mistake!'

Looking back to Will's camera again, Abigail said,

'This is Abigail Love, reporting from Turnpike Crescent, where it looks likely that there will shortly be a vacant post for Portsmouth and Gosport's Labour candidature.'

After fixing her normal smile at the camera, but only for a few seconds, she said to Will, 'Quick, let's get the fuck out of here, before they all start shooting!'

CHAPTER THIRTY THREE
ELECTION DAY BEGINS

A FEW WEEKS later, the day of the Portsmouth and Gosport by-election had arrived, and Hampshire Today's staff were assembling themselves for the start of their morning production meeting.

At the head of the table, as always, sat Eliot Bespoke, who was looking well, being that he didn't have a black eye anymore, his arm seemed to have healed, he'd shaved and was wearing clothes that hadn't been ripped, soiled or splattered with blood.

At his right hand sat his editor, Martin Grafham, who also seemed to have made a full recovery since what had become known as the UKIP Riot that he and Eliot had accidentally started. He'd also managed to shave, and was wearing a pressed suit with a clean shirt and tie. Furthermore, his neck was out of the brace that he'd been forced to wear for several weeks, which meant that he could now move his head around freely and without the constant pain he'd been previously subjected to.

'OK, people,' Eliot began. 'If you can settle down as quickly as possible, please.'

He was looking specifically at Abigail, who'd been the last to walk in, as was often the case, and was scouting the boardroom for a spare seat. She'd already spotted Will, but he'd not saved one for her, which was no great surprise. He'd not done so since that fateful evening down at the Badger and Hamster pub, all those weeks ago, when she'd screwed up by admitting to having known him from school. She stared over at him now as he read what looked like the Portsmouth Post. With his doleful brown eyes, dark hair and boyish good looks, she couldn't help but have a miserable feeling that she may just end up regretting what she'd told him for the rest of her life.

Just then, Jenny Daily, their fashion correspondent, caught her eye and offered her the seat next to hers. Abigail didn't mind at all. They had a decent enough relationship, although more so at the beginning of each month when Jenny received all the various fashion magazines that were sent over to her as part of her job.

They whispered hello, complimenting each other's hair and their morning's fashion accessory choices, until Eliot glared at them and called, 'Have we quite finished?'

Realising that he was referring to them, and that they'd been the only ones still talking, they each gave him an apologetic, albeit embarrassed nod, and decided that that was the perfect time to check through the contents of their handbags.

'OK, people,' repeated Eliot. 'Today's the day of the much anticipated Portsmouth and Gosport by-election, so unless anyone has got anything else that needs to be covered...?'

He left that sentence to hang, so it became more of an open question, just in case anyone did.

A tentative hand went up from the end of the table.

It was their sports correspondent, Malcolm McDonald.

'Yes, Malcolm?'

'They've still not found that teenage girl who went missing yesterday.'

'You mean the one who'd started that sponsored swim to the Isle of Wight?' asked Eliot.

'That's the one,' replied Malcolm.

'And that's still coming under the category of sport, is it?'

'I must admit that it's becoming an increasingly grey area,' admitted Malcolm. 'If she's still alive, and subsequently still swimming, then I guess it does. But for all other scenarios, probably not.'

'OK, but can't you give it a miss? I could really do with everyone focussing on the election.'

'Well yes, I could, I suppose, but I was hoping to be able to cover the story from the coastguard's perspective as the search for her continues, and it's unlikely they'll keep looking beyond the end of today.'

'I thought the general consensus of opinion was that she must have been run over by a ferry, and therefore it's unlikely that she'll be found. Not in one piece, that is.'

'That does seem to be the most popular theory, yes, although her parents are pinning their hopes on the notion that it could have all just been an elaborate stunt in order for her to elope.'

'What, with a *man*?'

'That's what they've told me, yes.'

'You have seen her picture, haven't you?' asked Eliot.

'It is rather unlikely, I know.'

'And she won't look any better if she's been run

over by a ferry.'

Malcolm just shrugged.

'That aside,' continued Eliot, 'I suppose you'd better cover it. But I suggest you do it from on board a ferry, not the coastguard's rescue boat. You'd then be able to interview the captain and ask what their policy is for when they see someone in the water. Personally, I've never heard of a ferry stopping to carry out a rescue attempt, which does seem a little odd now that I think about it. So it may be that it's their practice not to risk going off-schedule and just turn a blind eye to anyone they happen to see, running them over in the process. Even if they don't, it would make a good story.'

As Malcolm made a note of what his boss had said, Eliot looked around again, asking, 'Does anyone else need to cover something today, other than the election?'

Their crime correspondent, Declan Hacker, raised his hand.

'A dog's been found this morning.'

On hearing this most irregular announcement of good news, Martin was jolted out of the daydream he'd been having about catching a ferry to the Caribbean. 'Really?'

'Apparently, yes.'

'Do you know its name?'

Looking down at his notes, Declan replied, 'Pencil Case.'

'No, I'm sorry Declan,' interrupted Eliot, as he glanced from one to the other, 'but it's bad enough that we have to cover missing dogs, let alone found ones, and I'd rather have you on the election today.'

But Declan didn't mind at all. He'd been running stories about missing dogs for so long that he'd be happy if every one of them ended up inside a frozen lasagne.

'Anyone else?' asked Eliot.

Jim Oakburn, social affairs correspondent, lifted his hand.

'The Portsmouth Parents Association are opening the new HMS Victory Adventure Playground this afternoon.'

'Already?' asked Eliot. 'I thought they'd only just been given planning permission?'

'The council approved it last week,' continued Jim, 'but because they'd specified that the ship wasn't to be modified in any way, to open it all the parents had to do was to lay down some mats on the deck and nail up a sign.'

'But, surely,' interjected Martin, 'the Royal Navy has lodged some sort of official complaint at the idea of having children climbing all over what is probably the most famous ship in the world?' He'd heard the news that the council had caved in to parental pressure, but still couldn't quite believe it.

'Apparently not,' replied Jim. 'I've heard that they going to receive a percentage share of the playground's profits, and seem to be of the opinion that it will help to raise public interest in the Navy as being a sensible career option.'

'Well, OK,' said Eliot. 'You'd better cover it. Besides, it does sound highly likely that some poor child will get hurt, so just make sure that you're on the scene with your camera when they do!'

With that, Eliot stared around the room again.

'Is everyone else free to cover the election?'

Nobody responded either way, so he closed the subject by saying, 'Good,' and turned his mind to briefing them on how he thought the day would pan out, and subsequently where best to position them all.

'As you all know, with the arrest of Harold Webber there are only three runners left; Jane Marigold for the Green Party, John Smith for UKIP and Douglas McDongle for the Conservatives.'

At that moment, Abigail shot her hand into the air.

'Yes, Abigail?'

'I've been able to dig up some rather interesting information about our Mr McDongle,' she announced, before pausing for dramatic effect.

'Yes, and?' asked Eliot, hoping that it was nothing too salacious, as they were still supposed to be supporting his election campaign.

'Well,' she continued, 'I thought I recognised him from somewhere a few weeks back, but it took me a while to work out from where.'

She stopped again, and Eliot was forced to give her another prompt.

'Can you please hurry up, Abigail. We've still got a lot to get through.'

Apologising, she said, 'Yes, of course,' and continued. 'So anyway, I've since discovered that he is none other than...' another pause, before almost shouting out, '*MOROSE!*' just about as dramatically as she thought it was humanly possible to do, and in much the same way as she'd seen countless famous detectives do on both film and TV having solved yet another high profile murder case.

Everyone in the room gasped, as she'd hope they would, apart from Will of course, who already knew, and Eliot, who simply didn't believe her.

'Morose?' he asked.

'Yes!' she replied. 'None other than the former Chief Inspector of the Solent Police, the very man who became known as the Psychotic Serial Slasher of Southampton and the South Coast, and the same one who escaped from Portsmouth Prison and invaded the Isle of Wight!'

'And also the same man you found dead on the beach without a head?'

'The very same!' concluded Abigail.

'You are joking, I assume?' Eliot had heard a few tall tales in his time, most of which he'd made up himself, but this one really took the biscuit.

Ignoring his question, Abigail began to elaborate on her extraordinary discovery.

'I first became suspicious when I saw him give his speech at the Town Hall. That was when—'

'Look, Abigail, that's all fascinating, I'm sure, but do you have any actual proof that he's Morose, or is this just something you thought up on the way in?'

Abigail was a little taken aback by her boss's unusual negative attitude towards her story. He was normally considerably more willing to believe just about anything she came up with, and he'd certainly never asked her for proof before. But at least she'd had the foresight to hold off the announcement until she had the evidence she was clearly going to need.

From the depths of her handbag she heaved out the thermos flask that had been returned to her the day before, still in its clear plastic evidence bag, and still with the Solent Police label on it.

As everyone sat up to take a look at what she had, she continued, 'I have here a thermos flask that I asked Mr Douglas McDongle to hold after he'd knocked that old man off the bike.'

'I thought he'd rescued an old man who'd got knocked off his bike?' asked Jenny, sitting next to her.

'Er, yes. That *was* the story that we ran,' said Eliot, giving Martin a conspiratorial glance.

'Anyway,' said Abigail, who quite frankly didn't give a shit how her stories were manipulated to fit Hampshire Today's political agenda, 'I had Solent Police run a full fingerprint analysis of the flask, and they've come back to say that the prints are without a shadow of doubt, those of the former Chief Inspector Morose!'

A stunned silence fell around the table. Even Eliot looked shocked.

Eventually, Martin said, 'That's one hell of a story!'

He was right, and Eliot knew it. But he also knew that he now faced a serious dilemma. Assuming that McDongle was indeed the former Chief Inspector Morose, which did actually make good sense now that he thought about it, he'd have to tread very carefully. He'd made an agreement with the man that he'd run positive news items about him in the run up to the election in exchange for stories, and McDongle had certainly kept to his side of the bargain. But somehow he didn't think that running a story which announced that McDongle was actually the mass-murdering psycho nut-job Morose on the very day of the election would be seen as positive, not from McDongle's perspective at any rate. And Eliot really didn't fancy falling out of favour with him, probably because he'd end up dead, either through being buggered to death by the use of a well-endowed Eastern European gentleman and some superglue, or simple decapitation, a trick he must have used on that body down on the beach. Neither sounded particularly appealing.

He leaned back in his chair, entwined his fingers together and gazed up at the ceiling, as everyone in the room stared at him, waiting to hear what he'd have to say.

But then the answer dawned on him. All he had to do was to keep his promise, that being to support McDongle up until the election. He'd not said anything about what he said or did afterwards. On that thought, he leaned forward in his chair, looked over at Abigail and said, 'We'll run with it…'

Abigail gave him a beaming great smile.

'But,' he added, 'not until *after* the election!'

'But surely,' protested Abigail, 'if we run it today, then it will have a massive impact on the result?'

'It would,' agreed Eliot. 'However, he deserves to see if he can win it as who he is now. He has, after all, given us enough stories to cover all our salaries ten times over, and we owe him that much. And besides, I really don't think it will make any difference if we run it before or after. Either way, it will be absolutely huge!'

CHAPTER THIRTY FOUR
Confession Time

B EING THAT she was closest to the story, with all the other available Hampshire Today reporters left to wander the streets of Portsmouth in a forlorn bid to find someone who even knew that there was a by-election going on, let alone one who was willing to tell them who they'd voted for, Abigail, and her cameraman Will, had been given the prime location of the Town Hall. After all, that was where the ballot boxes were to be collected and votes counted, and that was where the winning candidate would be announced, closely followed by his or her acceptance speech.

But as exciting as all that may have sounded, it wasn't, and Abigail and Will had nothing better to do for the entire day other than stare at their iPhones, Abigail using hers to chat to her Facebook friends, and Will to play Star Wars: Galaxy Heroes.

As they were stuck in the same room, even if it was rather a large one, eventually, and after being unable to stop glancing over at him, Abigail worked up the courage to go and talk to Will, and about something other than decapitated bodies, penises superglued up inside middle-aged couples, Neo Nazi Labour candidates arrested on suspicion of both murder and kidnapping, and politically volatile flasks of coffee.

'How are you doing?' she asked him, as she took the empty chair next to his.

'All right,' he answered, a little pre-occupied as

227

Luke Skywalker battled Darth Vader between his thumbs.

'Is the Force with you?' she asked, having seen what he was playing. She'd meant it to have come out as the sort of question a fellow Star Wars fan would have asked, but it had come out more like she was just taking the piss.

The remark, together with the fact that she was sitting in such close proximity to him, made him lose his concentration, and as Darth Vader took off his son's head, Will gave up with the game, put his iPhone away and asked 'What is it that you want, exactly?'

'I just came over to say hello.'

'That's nice.'

'Look, Will, I'm really sorry about the other week, down at the pub, and all that other stuff.'

By "all that other stuff" she was, of course, referring to her psychological torture of him during their school days, but she wasn't going to make the mistake of bringing *that* up again!

'But I was really hoping we could start over.' She took a chance on further rejection by resting her hand gently on his thigh.

But the gesture was enough, and as Will began to warm to the moment, all the hostility he'd been forcing himself to hold against her since that evening down at the Badger & Hamster melted.

Without wanting to look into her eyes, he bowed his head and said, 'I'm sorry as well, Abi. But I, too, have a confession to make.'

Instinctively, Abigail withdrew her hand. *He IS gay!* she thought. *After all that, he's a bloody gay!*

'I wasn't exactly honest with you, back at the pub,' he continued.

Abigail didn't say anything, but just carried on staring at the side of his face, as she mentally prepared her response to his emergence from out of the closet by saying something like, *It's not your fault you're a gay, but you should have told me sooner!*

As Will took a deep breath, he eventually came out with what he should have said a long time before then. 'It's just that I, well, I *do* remember you from school.'

With relief that he hadn't just announced that he preferred men over women, Abigail relaxed a little.

'I recognised you the very first day we met,' he continued, 'when we were driving over to interview that policeman, the one who was in a coma.'

At first, Abigail still didn't say anything. It was good that he'd not come out to say that he was a gay, of course, but she couldn't help but feel like she'd been lied to, and worse, that if he'd know who she was all the way back then, he'd even slept with her knowing it, and without saying a word.

But then she remembered just how mean she'd been to him at school. And the fact that he *could* remember who she was, and that he hadn't said anything, must have meant that he must have liked her too.

So she decided that the time had most definitely come for a full apology. After all, the whole situation had been created by her, by being so unbelievably nasty to him for all those years.

'It's my fault,' she said, replacing her hand on his thigh. 'It's *all* my fault,' she repeated, as she felt the emotions that had been building up within her since that evening down the pub begin to break through from behind her eyes like an overflowing dam. 'I should've never said those things to you at school. I'm ashamed of myself for how I behaved. I know it won't make up for it, and it certainly doesn't justify what I said, b-but I only did say those things because, well, because I…I liked you.'

On hearing that, Will turned to face her.

'You…liked me?' he asked, with unhidden incredulity. 'At school, you, you…liked me?' he repeated.

It was Abigail's turn to stare down at the floor.

'I didn't just like you, Will. I *really* liked you. But I was just a stupid teenager with bad skin, yellow teeth and NHS glasses, and I honestly thought you'd not even look twice at me, so it was just the only thing I could think of to ever say.'

'You mean, calling me "Wee Willy Wankett", and asking me, over and over again, if I'd lost my blankett, was the only thing you could think of to say?' he asked.

Abigail nodded slowly, as her tears now ran freely down her cheeks and along the sides of her nose.

With a sigh deep enough to reach the bottom of the Atlantic Ocean, Will said, 'Well, as you said down at the pub, it was all a really long time ago,' and as he placed his hand on top of hers, he continued. 'I must admit, that I liked you too, *despite* everything you said.'

He gave her hand a gentle squeeze, and she turned to face him. As they looked deep into each other's eyes, he went on, 'And I still do.'

Abigail's tears of guilt turned to those of joy, and

Will helped her to wipe them all away. And now smiling at each other, they rubbed noses for one brief moment, and kissed.

CHAPTER THIRTY FIVE
NO COMMENT

A S DAY TURNED to night, after popping out into the car park to re-conjugate their relationship, and having ambled, arm-in-arm, down the road for some fish and chips, Abigail and Will arrived back just in time to see the ballot boxes being escorted in.

And not too far behind them were the remaining candidates, Jane Marigold for the Green Party, John Smith for UKIP, and Douglas McDongle for the Conservatives, along with a number of their loyal supporters, none of whom could do anything more to alter the course of the by-election than to simply wait for the votes to be counted. Even UKIP's leader, Michael Suntage, had turned up to offer his immoral support, and with the hopeful expectation of gaining another Parliamentary seat for his party.

Having seen the size and number of the black steel ballot boxes, Abigail had at first been concerned that the evening had only just begun, and that it would be many more hours before all the ballot papers had been counted. But she was pleasantly surprised to see that only a handful of voting slips fell out from each box. And so, she and Will cuddled up in the very back corner of the Town Hall to wait patiently for the results, along with everyone else.

They didn't have to wait long. About forty-five minutes later, various local dignitaries gathered on the wooden stage at the far end of the hall, and prepared themselves for the winner to be announced.

Noticing Will had dozed off, Abigail gave him a prod and whispered into his ear that it was time for them to get back to work.

With an impressive yawn, he clawed his iPhone from out of his inside suit jacket pocket and sat up to join Abigail.

'Thank you all for staying up so late,' said the same old man who'd introduced the candidates at the opening round of speeches. 'You'll be pleased to hear that despite having lost our Labour candidate, Mr Harold Webber, who's apparently helping the police with enquiries surrounding multiple murder and kidnapping, we've had a record turnout for the Portsmouth and Gosport by-election, with over five hundred people casting their votes.

A smattering of applause came from everyone in the room, as Will whispered over to Abigail, *'Is that a lot?'*

But Abigail didn't know, so she just shrugged.

'And now the time has come to announce the results,' continued the old man, glancing over at the candidates which must have been a signal for them to stand up from their chairs.

'Jane Marigold, for the Green Party.'

A pause followed as everyone waited to hear how many she'd picked up.

'Three votes.'

Surprisingly, Jane appeared to be delighted, and waved frantically to the crowd who made an effort to applaud her unparalleled lack of achievement.

'John Smith, for the United Kingdom Independence Party.'

Another pause.

'Two hundred and fifty seven votes.'

It was Mr Smith's turn to look as pleased as punch, as he waved frantically to the crowd who applauded him with more gusto.

Abigail leaned over to Will and whispered, *It's going to be close.'*

'And finally, Douglas McDongle for the Conservatives.'

The hall fell silent once again, as everyone sat forward in their seats to hear what would be the decider.

'Two hundred and fifty two votes.'

The UKIP supporters exploded with rapturous cheering and applause, so much so that the speaker had to raise his voice more than he'd have preferred, to say, 'I'm therefore forced to announce that the winner of the Portsmouth and Gosport by-election is John Smith for the United Kingdom Independence Party.'

As the applause continued, and as John Smith himself started to jump up and down on the stage like a middle-aged Sex Pistols fan who'd woken up to find himself in the wrong decade, but at least could buy *Never Mind the Bollocks* on CD, Abigail said, 'Our Mr Douglas McDongle doesn't look very happy.'

With the election now officially over, she pulled out her mobile to call Eliot, who'd asked her to phone the minute the results had been announced.

'Eliot, it's Abigail,' she said. 'It was close, but

McDongle lost to UKIP.'

She listened for a few moments, said, 'OK, we'll ask him,' and ended the call.

'C'mon,' she said to Will. 'We need to catch McDongle before he leaves.'

'Are you sure,' said Will. 'I mean, he looks seriously pissed off.'

'And therefore the perfect time to ask him about his true identity.'

'That would make it the worse time, surely?' asked Will, without budging from his seat.

But as Abigail had already started charging her way over to the stage, digging her microphone out from her handbag as she did, she left Will with little choice but to follow.

Leaping up onto the platform, she made a beeline straight for McDongle, who was now slumped in his chair, sneering over at the winning candidate.

As she approached, Abigail called out, 'Mr McDongle, Mr McDongle. Can we have a word, please?'

He transferred his glare to Abigail. Forcing himself up from his chair to rise above her like King Kong but without all the hair, he stared down at her with a look of malevolent intent.

'Er,' she said, beginning to feel just a little out of her depth, and glanced over her shoulder, hoping to see Will standing behind.

Fortunately for her, he was, but it was clear from the look on his face that he was already wishing he wasn't.

With renewed courage gained from having two of

them standing underneath the giant orange gorilla-shaped man, Abigail turned to face Will's camera, and speaking into her microphone, said, 'This is Abigail Love reporting from the Portsmouth and Gosport by-election, where Conservative candidate, Mr Douglas McDongle, has just been defeated by UKIP.' She turned to look back up at McDongle, asking, 'Mr McDongle, how do you feel about the result?' before holding up the microphone as high as she could for him to answer.

'Thrilled,' he said, through gritted teeth, and looking as if he was about to pick her up to use her as a toothpick.

Deciding not to dilly-dally for too long, and just in case he *did* have some food caught between his teeth, she moved in for what she sincerely hoped would be the killer question; and after a short intake of breath, asked, 'Do you think you'd have fared any better if you'd been representing the Conservative Party as the former Chief Inspector Morose?'

She lifted her microphone again to capture his response, but as his eyes had widened, his mouth hung open, and even some of the orange colour had drained from his face, his expression was answer enough. And as he took a step backwards, he asked. 'W-what do you mean?'

'If you were Chief Inspector Morose,' repeated Abigail, 'the man who became known as the Psychotic Serial Slasher of Southampton and the South Coast, the former Head of the Centre for Organised Crime and Kidnapping, and the same person who attempted to take over the Isle of Wight; if you were him, do you think you'd have been able to win the Portsmouth and Gosport by-election?'

She'd done her research well, and seemed to know all about who he'd been in his former life.

'I've n-no idea what you're t-talking about!' he stammered, taking another step backwards and now searching the room, seemingly desperate to spot an escape route large enough for him to fit through.

'Oh, I think you do,' continued Abigail, as Will carried on filming behind her.

But then McDongle paused, focussed his attention back on Abigail, and stepped towards her to lean down to have a more private word.

'You may *think* you do, Miss Love,' he said, speaking with a voice that was thick with dark ominous foreboding, 'but that doesn't mean that you do though, now does it?'

'I think it does, Mr McDongle, and I know that because I have evidence, verified by the Solent Police, that proves beyond a shadow of doubt that you are none other than the former Chief Inspector Morose!'

They continued to glare at each other for another few moments, before Abigail smiled at him and asked, 'Would you like to comment on that?'

But he didn't. He *really* didn't. And reaching the conclusion that she probably did have some evidence against him, shoved first her, and then Will, to the floor, and was off, frantically barging his way down from the stage and through the crowds, making good headway out towards the main doors at the back of the hall.

CHAPTER THIRTY SIX
A FISHERMAN'S FRIEND

RARELY HAD McDongle been so furious, not since he'd changed his identity at any rate. The whole world was clearly working against him and he was determined to make it pay, at least those UKIP types who must have somehow rigged the election in their favour. But at least he knew what he was going to do next.

Having borrowed Elizabeth's car again to get there, as she'd been unable to attend due to an urgent client meeting, he drove straight down to Harry Kari's Fishing & Hunting Centre, the same shop where he'd bought his gun and fishing rod. He'd remembered from his first visit there that they sold what he was after. They were an under-the-counter item, but Harry Kari's had offered them as part of the deal nonetheless, telling him that they were what every extreme fisherman would have died for, and absolutely ideal for those in a bit of a hurry: PE-4 plastic explosives! And although he'd not foreseen the need for any at the time, he was certainly keen to get his hands on some now.

Parking on the kerb outside the shop, he found them to be closed, which was hardly surprising, given that it was gone half-past ten. Making sure the street was clear of potential witnesses, he decided to open the shop himself by picking up a nearby brick and lobbing it through the door's window. And as the

238

shop's alarm pierced the silence of the Portsmouth night, he opened the door from the inside, being careful not to cut himself in the process, and crunched his way in over the broken glass, heading straight for the shop's sales counter, hoping they'd still be there.

And they were.

There wasn't a lot, but it was enough, and all packed carefully away inside a plain rectangular metal tin with an airtight lid. After prising off the top to have a quick check inside, he closed it back up and made good his escape before either a private security firm or, less likely but still possible, the Solent Police showed up.

It was then back to the Town Hall, where he parked opposite, just in time to see Michael Suntage emerge with his arm around UKIP's brand new Member of Parliament, Mr John Smith, along with numerous other of their party supporters.

McDongle's plan was simple: to follow them back to wherever it was that they were bound to have some sort of celebratory event, and then blow them all to Kingdom Come, somehow discarding his current identity in the process. Once that was done, he'd be able to rise from the ashes as yet another brand new person, by having a chat to the lady he now considered to be his long-term companion, who'd he effectively shacked up with: Elizabeth Potts.

After trailing what turned out to be a small convoy of cars back to what he assumed must be John Smith's place, a large Victorian detached house with red brick walls and an impressive drive, McDongle waited for them all to park up and pile inside.

Once the front door closed, he opened up the tin of explosives to find the instructions. They were simple enough. He just had to set the digital timer for the acquired amount of time and press ENTER.

Without giving it too much thought he buried the fuse into the 2.5 kg of PE-4 plastic explosive, set the digital timer up for ten minutes and pushed the ENTER button, as instructed. Then he thought that he could easily need more time to deliver the package and get back to the car before the whole thing went off, so he pressed RESET, and changed it back to twenty minutes. Pressing ENTER again he was just about to replace the lid, when he changed his mind. Twenty minutes was far too long, and it could easily give those inside the house time to discover what it was and clear the building before it had a chance to do what he hoped it would, and kill them all. So he pressed the RESET button again, changed it back to ten minutes and replaced the lid. He then squeezed himself out of the car, and carrying the tin in front of him as if it were the ashes of some dear departed colleague, crossed the road and weaved his way past all the executive cars scattered over the drive, and climbed the six steps to the front door.

He rang the bell.

After waiting for what seemed like an eternity, but which was probably more like thirty seconds, McDongle changed his mind again, and now wished he'd set the timer for twenty minutes. He could hear the sound of people having what must be a great time inside, but nobody was coming to the door.

He rang the bell again, but this time with more

perseverance.

That must have done the trick, as he could already hear footsteps approach. The door was opened, and McDongle found himself greeted by none other than John Smith himself.

'Hello, John,' said McDongle, giving him a magnanimous smile.

'Oh, er, hello. Douglas, isn't it?' asked John, feeling rather awkward.

'I just wanted to pop round to congratulate you on your win,' continued McDongle. 'And by way of saying well done, and that there are no hard feelings, I thought I'd give you a little something.'

With that, he handed the tin over to John before taking half a step away from it.

'Gosh!' exclaimed John. 'Thank you very much,' and with clear excitement at having been given an actual present, and before John could suggest otherwise, he prised open the lid and stared inside.

McDongle took another half-step backwards.

'What is it?' asked John, who'd never seen a real-life bomb before.

'Oh, er...' began McDongle, trying to think of something it could be, but without saying what it actually was. 'It's a, er...cake!' he said, and gave the new UKIP Member of Parliament an honest sort of a grin.

'Really?' asked John. 'I must admit that it looks more like...well, I suppose it looks a bit like what I'd have thought a bomb might look like.'

Thinking fast, McDongle said, 'Remarkable, isn't it? They can make cakes look like almost anything these days!'

'Wow! Yes! That really *is* good,' agreed John. 'And thank you very much!'

'It's my pleasure,' McDongle replied, as he took another step backwards. 'Anyway,' he continued, 'I really must be off now, but, er, well done again, and, um…good luck with the, er…' and couldn't help but glance down at the tin. Thinking it best to leave it at that, he gave the man a final wave and turned to lumber his way as quickly as his vast physical mass would allow, towards the relative safety of his car.

'Thanks again!' John called, and with a beaming great smile, replaced the tin's lid and disappeared back inside the house, closing the front door behind him.

The moment McDongle heard the door close, he stopped dead in his tracks.

'Shit!' he said, out loud, but to nobody in particular.

He'd forgotten about his plan to leave his wallet behind at the scene.

Without wasting another moment, he turned around and headed back towards the front door, removing his wallet from his inside suit jacket pocket as he did so.

As soon as he reached it, he popped the wallet through the letter box, and then did his very best to run back to his car without having a cardiac arrest in the process.

Once there, he took shelter behind the Nissan Micra, as he caught his breath and waited for what he hoped would be the inevitable giant explosion with both trepidation and glee.

But he was still there, ten minutes later, staring at

his watch.

He stood up with some caution to glare over at the house.

'Fucking thing,' he said out loud, checking his watch for the umpteenth time. *It definitely should have gone off by now,* he thought. *Maybe I set the timer wrong? Or maybe they worked out what it was and were somehow able to defuse it?*

Having decided that he'd definitely set it for ten minutes, and that even if they had realised that it was a bomb, and not a cake made to look like one, then he'd have seen everyone run out of the house screaming a long time before some brave soul had a go at trying to defuse it. And even then, they'd have still called the police, and he couldn't even hear the sound of an approaching police car, let alone see one tearing up the road towards him.

He re-checked his watch again.

'Fuck it,' he said, and sighed as he looked back over towards the house.

He realised that it did seem a little quiet, and wondered if maybe they'd taken it down to the cellar, and perhaps it had gone off there?

There was nothing for it, he was going to have to take a look. So he stepped around the car, glanced both ways before re-crossing the road, and tentatively weaved his way back around all the cars still parked on the drive, ducking behind each one as he did. But as still nothing had gone bang, not to his knowledge at least, when he reached the porch steps he took them two at a time before taking shelter behind the wall, alongside the solid oak front door. There he listened again, but he still couldn't hear the sounds of a party going on as he'd done before.

What the fuck is going on? he thought to himself, and taking to one knee, pushed open the letterbox to peer inside.

It was still there, on the hall table, under a mirror. But where had everyone else gone?

But he didn't get the chance to find out. In his haste to take out his revenge on UKIP and the world in general, although he'd re-set the timer back to ten minutes, he'd neglected to press the ENTER button, so it was still set to twenty.

As the bomb exploded, the blast ripped the front door out of its frame and sent it flying about twenty feet backwards to land on the top of a black Series 7 BMW parked in the middle of John Smith's driveway, with McDongle still trying to peek through the letterbox underneath it, albeit with his eyes closed.

CHAPTER THIRTY SEVEN
CAREER CHOICES

A BIGAIL AND WILL had only just arrived back at her place to see if Will was up to having another go at re-conjugating their relationship, but this time on a warm comfortable bed, and not up against the Town Hall's industrial-sized wheelie bin, when her mobile phone rang.

It was Eliot, asking if they wouldn't mind popping out to cover the story of what appeared to be a terrorist attack on the home of the newly elected John Smith.

Initially she declined, probably because she'd only just removed her bra, and Will was massaging her breasts as she took the call. As Will gazed at them with a look of wondrous hedonistic astonishment, she was looking forward to what he was going to do next. But when Eliot told her that an immensely fat bald-headed man had been caught in the explosion and had ended up on top of a car, underneath the front door of the building that had been bombed, hoping it was who she thought it was, she'd told Will that they were going to have to wait for another hour or so.

With no traffic to contend with, they were at the scene within fifteen minutes of having received the call, and they found the emergency services in full swing. Firemen were attempting to put out the flames still sprouting from what was left of a large detached Victorian house, paramedics were helping charred victims to crawl out from the ruins, the police were interviewing those who could still hear enough of what was being asked of them to answer, and the AA was assisting those who were up for driving home to re-start their cars and replace any tyres that had been punctured by the blast.

With so much going on, Abigail didn't know quite where to start, but then she saw a crowd who'd gathered around a black BMW that had a wooden door lying on its roof, and what looked like a giant orange slug wearing a suit lodged under that.

McDongle! she thought.

'C'mon,' she said to Will, punching his arm as she did.

'Ow,' he said, wondering if she was always going to be like this, or if she'd calm down if they got married and had children. Leaving such thoughts for another time, he retrieved his trusty iPhone and hurried along after.

Pulling out her microphone, Abigail charged over towards the car on top of which McDongle lay, under what she assumed used to be the building's front door. 'Mr McDongle! Mr McDongle!' she called out. 'How does it feel to have been blown up?'

But the moment the police contingent of those gathered around the car saw her approach, they temporarily gave up trying to work out how they were going to lift the front door off of the giant of a man who'd somehow managed to survive the blast, without injuring him further in the process, and the three of them formed a human barrier to prevent her from going any closer.

That didn't stop her from continuing to ask McDongle a series of questions, as she attempted to fight her way through the human police blockade.

'Mr McDongle, what were you doing here? Did you have anything to do with the explosion? Are you a terrorist bomber as well as the former Chief Inspector of the Solent Police? Was this a deliberate attempt to eliminate the UKIP party single-handedly, or were you simply trying to tell them that you didn't approve of their stance on immigration? Did you blow yourself up by accident, Mr McDongle, or was this a failed attempt to take your own life?'

As the policemen began shoving her back out towards the street, and away from the man she was persisting in questioning even though it must have been obvious to the most casual observer that he'd have a real struggle to respond, she eventually gave up. The three of them were just too strong for her and as long as they remained, it was unlikely that she'd get the exclusive interview she was looking for. So she said, 'Alright boys, alright! You can stop pushing me now. I've got what I came for, thank you very much.'

After the policemen backed away, she called out to them, 'But you should know that that man there, on top of that car, is none other than your former Chief Inspector, Morose; the Psychotic Serial Slasher of Southampton and the South Coast, and the Head of the Centre for Organised Crime and Kidnapping. So, if I were you, I'd keep a very close eye on him!'

'Of course he is, miss,' said the tallest of the three policemen with a condescending smile.

'It's true!' she insisted. 'He really is Morose!' and

she pointed at him, just in case there was any confusion as to who she was referring to.

'Whatever you say,' said the same policeman. 'Now if you can move along please.'

As Abigail muttered, *'Moron,'* under her breath, she turned back to Will, who'd been filming for the entire time. And after a quick prod of her hair and a lick of her teeth, she stared at his iPhone and began her commentary for the story.

'This is Abigale Love, reporting from outside the home of UKIP's latest Member of Parliament, Mr John Smith, where it would appear that the man who's been going around calling himself Douglas McDongle, but who is really the escaped mass-murdering convict, Morose, has now turned his hand to terrorism. However, as he's managed to end up under a front door on top of a car, it looks like he's made a bit of a hash of it.

'But with Christmas fast approaching, and in the spirit of good will to all men, even psychotic mass-murdering ones, I'd like to suggest that, assuming he's still alive, and after he's finished what will be yet another series of back-to-back life sentences for murder, our Mr Morose should maybe try his hand at another profession.

'This is Abigail Love, reporting for Hampshire Today. Back to the studio.'

CHAPTER THIRTY EIGHT
A PROBLEM OF LOGISTICS

FEELING GUILTY that she'd not been able to attend the election results at the Town Hall, and even more so when she'd heard that McDongle had lost, Elizabeth had been waiting for him to come home with a large glass of port already poured out for him.

She'd become surprisingly fond of the man she now called Dougie since becoming his election agent. She didn't know why. He wasn't exactly the most attractive person in the world, although he did look better now that he was dressing well, had a healthy-looking tan and his teeth had been whitened. But other than his looks, he clearly had a few issues. The most obvious one was that he did seem to be permanently morose, though she could hardly blame him for that, as he must have spent the vast majority of his life with everyone calling him so. But it was his headstrong nature that she found most annoying. That, and the nasty habit he seemed to have picked up of murdering people, often unintentionally. She'd had strong words with him about it, especially when he'd admitted to her that he'd been responsible for shooting those three residents at Turnpike Crescent.

Despite warning him about what might happen if Harold Webber wasn't able to take part in the election, by either being locked up or permanently put out of action, Douglas had gone ahead and tried to kill him anyway. And what had been the result? Harold had been arrested for suspicion of murder and Douglas had lost the election to UKIP, just as she'd predicted!

But nobody was perfect, and she was hardly of the age where she could afford to be choosy about her men, especially when taking her own criminal background into account. And although nothing had been agreed, or even spoken of, she'd been delighted when he'd effectively moved in with her, which had been a remarkably straight forward process, and nothing like what most couples of a certain age would have had to have gone through. This was because, apart from a handful of clothes, he didn't seem to own much of anything. The only thing he did own, sort of, was a yacht, and he'd had that moored up in Trafalgar Wharf, shortly after he'd picked up his new identity.

So, with all that in mind, she'd been expecting him home that night, after the election results, and was naturally concerned when he didn't return.

Doing her best not to worry, and thinking that he'd probably slunk back to his yacht to wallow in self-pity with the aid of a bottle of scotch, she'd gone to bed. It was only at dawn the next morning, realising that she'd still not heard from him and after checking through her Facebook newsfeed, that she learnt about the bombing, and that Dougie, or McDongle as they'd referred to him, was under arrest in hospital for suspicion of being the bomber.

After phoning Portsmouth Hospital to find out if that was where he'd been taken, and to confirm that he was still alive, which he was, she dressed and did her hair and makeup just as quickly as possible before calling a cab to take her straight there.

Reception told her which room he was in, and she eventually found it on the fourth floor, along a pleasant carpeted corridor that had numerous wooden doors all the way down one side, and large double-glazed windows along the other. She wasn't at all surprised to see a policeman standing outside the one that McDongle was supposed to be in.

Fortunately for her, the young-looking constable hadn't been given any specific orders to not let anyone in, but only to make sure that McDongle didn't get out. He was happy to let Elizabeth in to see him, especially after she'd told him that she was McDongle's wife.

On entering the small room, despite the fact that it was dark as the curtains had yet to be opened, McDongle was easy enough to spot. At first she thought he must have died during the night, as he was facing up at the ceiling with his eyes closed, showing no obvious signs of life. However, she soon heard the gentle rhythmic bleeping sound that emanated out from one of the machines that she assumed was monitoring his heart. On closer inspection she was comforted to see that his mammoth chest was moving gently up and down.

So she pulled up a nearby chair, eased herself next to his charred but still predominantly orange head, and leaned in so that she could whisper gently into his ear.

'Dougie, it's me - Elizabeth!' she said. *'Can you hear me?'*

There was no response, and unable to think of anything else to say, asked, *'How are you feeling?'*

McDongle's eyes flickered open, and without

moving anything other than his mouth, said, 'Really well, thank you.'

'Oh, poor Dougie!' exclaimed Elizabeth, forced to assume that he was being sarcastic. Her heart went out to him, and she found herself unable to hold back the tears; but she wasn't going to allow herself to become emotionally overwhelmed by the situation, no matter how distressing she was finding it, and with firm resolve said, 'Don't worry my darling, I'm here for you now, and I'm going to take care of you, I *promise!*'

A single tear appeared in the corner of Douglas's eye. He'd clearly been touched by the gesture. Either that or he had something in it, but couldn't move his arms or hands to help get it out.

'Right!' said Elizabeth, and with her mind made up that she was going to look after him, no matter what, her brain kicked into gear as to how she'd be able to do that.

'The first thing we need to do is to get you out of here,' she said, looking over towards the door. 'Somewhere safe, and away from all those pesky policemen.'

She looked down at his whale-shaped body and couldn't help but wonder how they'd been able to get him into the room in the first place, let alone how she was going to get him out again.

But then she thought, *if I can't get him out, then I'll just have to do the next best thing.*

Having come up with a solution, she gave his hand a reassuring pat.

'I've got an idea, Dougie. You just take it easy, and I'll be right back.'

With that, she got up, and went over to the machine that was monitoring his heart, looking for an on/off switch. But she couldn't find one, so she glanced around behind it where she saw a socket in the wall. Making sure she had the right plug by tracing the cable back to the machine, she switched it off. Straight away it stopped making its regular beeping sound, causing Elizabeth to spin around to check that McDongle's chest was still moving up and down as it had been doing before. It was, so reassured that she hadn't turned off anything vital, she walked over to the door and eased it open.

'Excuse me,' she said to the policeman, still standing outside, 'but would you mind finding a doctor for me? It's just that I think my husband may have passed away during the night.'

The policeman didn't seem too surprised, and casually looked over her shoulder where he could just about make out McDongle, lying motionless on his back. But as he couldn't hear the regular bleeping noise that he'd heard when he'd first started his shift, he assumed that the lady was probably right. Even if she wasn't, and he was still alive, he was hardly concerned that he'd be in a condition to sneak out, not after he'd heard the stories of how many people it had taken to get him in!

Feeling nothing but sorrow for the lady, who must now be a widow, and delighted to have an excuse to go for a walk and stretch his legs, he said, 'I'll see if I can find someone for you,' and ambled away to do just that.

As soon as she'd seen him disappear around the

corner, Elizabeth popped back inside, took the clipboard off the end of McDongle's bed and headed back out into the corridor.

After checking that the coast was clear, she skulked over to the room next door and peaked inside. On the bed was another patient, so she closed the door and tried the next room along. There she found what she'd been looking for: an empty room!

She hurried in, closed the door, and went straight over to the bed to draw back the covers and give the pillows a few hefty thumps with her fist. She pulled the chair that was there over to the bed, to make it look like she'd been sitting in it. That done, she swapped the clipboard hanging off the edge of the bed for McDongle's, and using the pen lodged under the clip, copied the signature at the bottom onto that room's blank medical form. Finally, she went over to the windows and drew the curtains, plunging the room into semi-darkness, before heading back to the door.

Once there, she removed her purse from her handbag, slipped out a credit card and carefully opened the door to peer out into the corridor. Having checked down both sides, she used the edge of the card to remove the door's number 6 from what was room 436. That done, she raced back to McDongle's door, and using the same method, removed the number 4 from 434, sticking the 6 in its place. It didn't stick all that well, but she thought it would do, for now, and at least until she could return with some glue.

After taking the spare number 4 to the other room's door, and having stuck that on where the 6 had been, as best she could again, she rushed back to

McDongle's room.

Closing the door behind her, she took a moment to catch her breath before remembering to switch McDongle's heart monitoring machine back on. Then she sat down beside him again, and busied herself filling out the rest of his new medical form, giving him the temporary name of Henry Morgan, that being the first one that popped into her head. Presented with a blank space where the medical notes were supposed to have been recorded, she paused for a moment before writing, *"Fireman who's become too obese to do his job. Also suffering from acute depression. Gastric band to be fitted, followed by a six month term of psychiatric counselling."*

CHAPTER THIRTY NINE
IMPORTANT NEWS

'CAN YOU ALL settle down please? We've got a lot to get through.'

It was the beginning of that morning's production meeting at Hampshire Today, which Eliot had been forced to start late as he'd had to wait for Abigail and Will to come back from the hospital, where'd they'd been covering the story that McDongle had somehow managed to inexplicably vanish.

'Now, before we get started,' continued Eliot, 'I have a couple of important announcements to make.'

He waited for everyone to wind up their various conversations.

'The first is that, after what's been a truly amazing few weeks, during which time she's managed to pull in some quite extraordinary news stories, and – judging by what she's come back with this morning – continues to do so, it's my very great pleasure to announce that we've decided to promote Abigail up to the position of Special News Correspondent!'

Abigail nearly fell off her chair, and with Will giving her a proud smile, everyone else in the room turned to face her to offer their own congratulations; after all, their boss was right. She *had* somehow managed to bring in some quite remarkable stories since that day the headless body had been found down on the beach.

Raising both hands to ask for quiet, Eliot continued.

'But I'd also like to thank all of you. As a start-up YouTube news channel, I know that it must have felt like you were taking a bit of a gamble when you signed up with us. And thanks to all your hard work, we're doing better than I could have ever imagined, and you can all look forward to receiving what I hope will be the first of many quarterly bonuses at the end of the month.

There was a buzz around the room, as everyone smiled at each other, hoping that the bonus hinted at would be more than a £10 YouGet gift voucher.

'And that leads me to my next announcement.'

Silence fell back over the boardroom.

'Now, this may come as a bit of a shock to many of you, and before I say what it is, I want to reassure you all that we hope this will have a minimum impact on your current situations.'

He paused, not for dramatic effect, but more because he was a little nervous as to how his staff would react to what he had to say next.

As they all sat forward in their chairs, he pushed on.

'We've decided, after much deliberation, that we're going to change our name to Prime Time Today!'

On hearing the news, and with the build-up it had had, everyone just looked around at each other and shrugged.

But Eliot hadn't quite finished, and did so by adding, 'Oh, and we're going to be relocating up to London as well.'

'TO LONDON!' exclaimed the entire room, almost in unison.

Abigail and Will gazed around at each other, both

in complete shock.

'Yes, to London,' confirmed Eliot. 'But please, don't worry! We've absolutely no intention of making any of you redundant. In fact, we're sincerely hoping that you'll all be able to join us up there.'

As various people in the room began lifting their hands either to raise an objection or to ask a question, Eliot pre-empted what he thought they might be thinking.

'I know that many of you will be worried about how you'll be able to afford to live up there, and for good reason!'

He was right. That had been what most of them were going to ask.

'But with the move will come an across-the-board pay increase, to ensure that your salaries are in-line with those of the capital, and to help you all to afford to make the move.'

Noticing that some people's hands were still in the air, Eliot continued to try and placate them.

'Now, obviously, some of you will still have questions relating to your own personal circumstances, and I'll be more than happy to discuss those with you in private, but this won't be happening overnight, so we'll have plenty of time to make what I hope will be a smooth transition. But, for now, I'd just like to say that I see this as a tremendous opportunity for us to both expand and grow, and in a way that we simply can't do down here, in Portsmouth. So I'd like to leave it at that for the moment, if I may, and push on with our production meeting.'

But even before he'd stopped talking, all those in

attendance had begun discussing the news with each other, asking if they'd be willing to relocate.

Abigail was no different, and looked at Will to ask, 'How would you feel about moving up to London?'

Will looked into Abigail's eyes, and said, 'As long as you're there, I'm not sure I'd mind.'

She returned a warm, loving smile.

'Perhaps we could get a place together?' she suggested, and rested her hand on the upper part of his thigh.

He looked down at her hand, and moved it up a little, saying, 'Sounds good to me!'

Delighted with his response, and with everyone else in the room still absorbed in the discussion of Eliot's news, she leaned in towards him to steal herself a kiss, as she thought about where in London they'd be moving to, if they'd be able to afford a two bedroom flat with a half-decent kitchen, if it would come with a gas hob, a free-standing fridge freezer, and a dishwasher; and if she'd be able to convince her best friend, Sally Davies, to move up with them as well.

FIND OUT WHERE IT ALL BEGAN...

Who is Inspector Capstan, how did he end up in a coma, and why was the former Chief Inspector Morose forced to fake his own death to become Mr Douglas John McDongle?

Get the backstory with the **Inspector Capstan Series**.

ABOUT THE AUTHOR

ORN in a US Navy hospital in California, David
spent the first eight years of his life being
transported from one country to another, before
ending up in a three bedroom semi-detached house in
Devon, on the South Coast of England.

David's father, a devout Navy Commander, and his
Mother, a loyal Christian missionary, then decided to
pack him off to an all-boys boarding school in Surrey,
where they thought it would be fun for him to take up
ballet. Once there, he showed a remarkable aptitude
for dance and, being the only boy in the school to
learn, found numerous opportunities to demonstrate
the many and varied movements he'd been taught,
normally whilst fending off attacks from his classroom
chums who seemed unable to appreciate the skill
required to turn around in circles, without falling over.

Meanwhile, his father began to push him down the
more regimented path towards becoming a trained
assassin, and spent the school holidays teaching him
how to use an air rifle. Over the years, and with his
father's expert tuition, he became a proficient
marksman, managing to shoot a number of things
directly in the head. His most common targets were
birds but also extended to those less obvious,
including his brother, sister, an uncle who popped in
for tea, and several un-suspecting neighbours caught
doing some gardening.

Horrified by the prospect of her youngest son
spending his adult life travelling the world to

indiscriminately kill people, for no particular reason, his mother intensified her efforts for him to enter the more highbrow world of the theatre by applying him to enter for the Royal Ballet. But after his twenty minute audition, during which time he jumped and twirled just as high and as fast as he possibly could, the three ballet aficionados who'd stared at him throughout with unhidden incredulity, proclaimed to his proud mother that the best and only role they could offer him would be that of, "Third Tree from the Left" during their next performance of Pinocchio, but that would involve him being cut down, with an axe, during the opening scene. Furthermore, they'd be unable to guarantee his safety as the director had decided to use a real axe instead of the normal foam rubber one, to add to the drama of an otherwise rather staid production.

A few weeks later, and unable to find any suitable life insurance, David's mother gave up her dream for him to become a famed primo ballerino and left him to his own devices.

And so it was, that with a sense of freedom little before known, he enrolled himself at a local college to study Chain Smoking, Under-Age Drinking, Drug Abuse and Fornication but forgot all about his core academic subjects. Subsequently he failed his 'A' Levels and moved to live in a tent in Dorking where he picked up with his more practised skills whilst working as a barbed wire fencer.

Having being able to survive the hurricane of '87, the one that took down every tree within a fifty mile radius of his tent, he felt blessed, and must have been destined for greater things, other than sleeping rough during the night and being repeatedly stabbed by hard to control pieces of metal during the day. So he talked his way onto a Business Degree Course at the University of Southampton.

After three years of intensive study and to the surprise of just about everyone, he graduated with a 2:1 and spent the next ten years working in several incomprehensibly depressing sales jobs in Central London, before setting up his own recruitment firm.

Seven highly profitable years later, during which time he married and had two children, the Credit Crunch hit, which ended that particular episode of his career.

It's at this point he decided to become a writer which is where you find him now, happily married and living in London with his young family.

When not writing he spends his time attempting to persuade his wife that she really doesn't need to buy the entire contents of Ikea, even if there is a sale on. And when there are no items of flat-packed furniture for him to assemble he enjoys writing, base-jumping, and drawing up plans to demolish his house to build the world's largest charity shop.

www.david-blake.com

Printed in Great Britain
by Amazon